From the Files of

Madison Finn

Read all the books about Madison Finn!

Coming Soon!

From the Files of Madison Finn

Lights Out!

By Laura Dower

HYPERION
New York

For Helen Perelman, editor, friend, and uber-babe

Text copyright © 2003 by Laura Dower

From the Files of Madison Finn, Volo, and the Volo colophon are trademarks of Disney Enterprises, Inc.

Printed in the United States of America

First Edition
3 5 7 9 10 8 6 4

The main body of text of this book is set in 13-point Frutiger Roman.

ISBN 0-7868-1686-4

Visit www.madisonfinn.com

Chapter 1

The clock on Mr. Sweeney's classroom wall buzzed like a wasp. For the first time this spring, the room was hot. Madison picked at a plastic tab on her math notebook and stared at the clock's hands, praying for them to turn ahead. Could one long and steady glare move time forward?

Nope.

Instead, the minute hand clicked backward.

Madison blinked, but it was truer than true. She was trapped in a math-class time warp, and there was nothing she could do about it!

Mr. Sweeney had his back to everyone. He was drawing geometric shapes on the blackboard and asking for class participation. The only kid who answered him was Wayne Ennis, math superwhiz.

But Mr. Sweeney was looking for *other* volunteers—like the kids who weren't paying attention.

Madison tried to avoid his darting eyes. Head down, she traced a few words in the margin of her notebook.

Jasper Woods. Field Trip. Wow.

She couldn't get her mind off the seventh-grade field trip that would be starting the next day. All the kids were traveling overnight to Jasper Woods, a camp located about two hours from Far Hills. It was a very big deal. Principal Bernard explained to students that the trip was for "personal growth and community experience," but Madison thought differently. It was a chance for boys and girls to be out of school for two days.

As she doodled hearts around the edge of the page, Madison daydreamed about what she and her best friends, Aimee Gillespie and Fiona Waters, would do together on the field trip. She wished they were in class right now to swap ideas, but unfortunately her BFFs were in a different math section.

"Maddie!" Egg whispered from the next row. He was Madison's best guy friend at Far Hills Junior High. His real name was Walter, but no one really called him that except for his mother and a few teachers, Mr. Sweeney included. Egg had just been transferred into Madison's math section.

"WALTER DIAZ!" Mr. Sweeney barked, facing the class. "Since you're so eager to speak, why don't *you*

do this problem on the board for us?" he asked.

Egg sank into his chair and turned crimson. He glanced back at Madison, who looked immediately to her right to keep from laughing.

From a seat behind, one of Madison's classmates, Lindsay Frost, snickered. "Looks like Egg is in trouble again," she said.

Madison quietly and carefully tore an edge off her notebook page and scribbled a secret note back to Lindsay.

> Are you packed 4 tomorrow?
> What r u wearing?
> Write back now or l8r.

She leaned over and tossed the note onto Lindsay's shoe. Fortunately, Mr. Sweeney missed the toss. He was too busy torturing Egg up at the board.

After a few more problems, math class finally ended. Egg grabbed his books and hustled out without glancing back. Madison headed for the door with Lindsay.

Near the exit, Ivy Daly and her drones, Joan and Rose, otherwise known as Phony Joanie and Rose Thorn, stood blocking the way.

"Look who's standing by the door," Lindsay said.

"Yeah," Madison whispered into Lindsay's ear. "Just waiting to ambush Mr. Sweeney on the way out. Pathetic. They'll do anything for a good grade."

As they approached, Madison heard Ivy and her friends gabbing about the field trip.

"I have to bring my new camera to Jasper Woods." Ivy snorted. "And my hair dryer, of course."

Her drone Joan snorted right back. "And don't forget the curling iron, too, right? You wanna look good for you-know-who."

Madison knew who "you-know-who" was. Hart Jones, the same seventh grader Madison liked.

"Um . . . you guys?" Madison said. Even though she shouldn't have been listening, Madison couldn't resist interrupting. "We're sleeping in a cabin. I don't think they allow hair dryers in the woods, Ivy."

"Of course they allow them," Ivy said with a huff. "They have electric sockets in the Jasper Woods facilities. And you would know that if you read your permission slip. Duh. Who invited you into our conversation, anyhow?"

"Yeah," Joan piped up. "No one invited *you*."

"Whatever," Madison said. She whirled around and grabbed Lindsay's elbow. "Let's go."

"Don't forget to pack your teddy bears," Joan taunted.

"Yeah, you don't want to get homesick or anything," Ivy added, cracking herself up.

Madison wished she could haul off and sock Ivy in the jaw, but she kept her cool. Thankfully Mr. Sweeney walked over before the drones could say more.

"They make me so-o-o mad," Madison grumbled as she and Lindsay walked away.

"Yeah, me too," Lindsay agreed.

"They treat us like idiots!" Madison grunted.

"Yeah," Lindsay said with a sigh.

But Madison had to admit: there was some truth in what the enemy said. Madison had never been to Jasper Woods or any other woods, for that matter. She'd never even been away to summer camp. Sure, she'd been traveling with Mom, a film producer for Budge Films. And in fourth grade she'd won a pink ribbon from Camp Chipachu, but that was just a day camp. That didn't count. Madison had never been to real sleep-away camp like all of her friends had.

Lindsay said good-bye quickly as they exited the classroom. She had to get to a photography club meeting. Madison dragged herself down the hall-way toward her locker. She hoped to find her BFFs waiting there. Maybe they could all walk home together.

Fiona leaned up against the wall with arms crossed, tapping her foot.

"I am so stressed!" Fiona cried when she saw Madison approach. "Egg just ignored me. He raced by and wouldn't even stop when I called after him. He won't talk to me!"

Madison sighed. Fiona always acted like a worry-wart when it came to Egg. She'd been crushing on him since the start of seventh grade. Sometimes it felt weird to be friends with people who liked each other like *that*.

Fiona rolled her eyes. "I just don't understand him," she said.

Aimee appeared at her side. "You don't understand *Egg*?" Aimee said with a chuckle. "Nobody understands Egg, Fiona. Except maybe Madison. . . ."

"Yeah, but—" Fiona started to say.

"Be quiet, you guys," Madison said. "He's coming."

Egg strutted back toward them, and he wasn't walking alone. Right behind him were Drew Maxwell, Egg's best pal; Chet, Fiona's twin brother; Dan Ginsburg, Madison's pal from school and the animal clinic; and Hart.

Madison bit her lip. Hart was wearing a rugby shirt with blue and gold stripes and khaki pants. She noticed how his brown hair was getting long on top. It whooshed over his forehead. She wished she could touch it—just once.

"Hey, you dorks!" Chet called out, ruining Madison's daydream.

Fiona turned in toward the locker. She pretended to be rifling through her bag for a pen.

"Hey, Finnster," Hart said, giving Madison a little punch on her shoulder. She blushed. Only Hart called her by that nickname.

"Hey, yourself," Madison answered.

"You guys psyched for the trip?" Aimee asked the group.

Fiona turned around meekly, eyes on Egg.

Egg didn't seem to notice.

"This trip is so lame," Chet declared. "Hanging around in some cabins . . . what's that?"

"I think the trip will be fun," Dan said.

"Well, we don't have classes," Aimee said.

"Maddie, are you bringing your laptop?" Egg asked.

"We can't bring laptops! You know that," Madison said.

"Yeah," Fiona added, trying to get into the conversation—and to get Egg's attention.

"I have to get to my ballet class," Aimee said, checking her watch. "Want to walk out together?" she asked Fiona and Madison.

"I don't know. Maddie, are you going home?" Fiona said, stalling to see if maybe Egg was doing something interesting.

Madison shrugged. "I guess," she said, anxious to see what *Hart* might be doing next.

"I'm out of here," Egg said, giving Hart and Drew both high fives. "I have to go meet my mom."

Egg's mother, Señora Diaz, taught Spanish at Far Hills Junior High. Some days she gave Egg and his friends a ride home. Drew and Hart asked if they could get a lift today, and Egg agreed. They wandered off down the hall together.

Fiona stared down the hall until Chet smacked her on the back.

"Fiona!" he cried. "Let's get going. Dad is picking us up out front, remember?"

"Don't *hit* me!" Fiona barked, smacking Chet right back.

Madison wondered why Egg hadn't stopped to talk to Fiona like he always did. Was their crush crushed? Was Hart acting hot and cold, too?

"I'm sorry, Maddie," Fiona said, changing her tone of voice. "I'd give you a ride, but Dad is taking us to the computer store."

"No problem," Madison said. "E me later."

Aimee slammed her locker. "I'm so late!" she said, spinning around. "I'll e you both after ballet!"

Waving good-bye, Madison watched Aimee twirl down the hall and through a set of swinging doors. Fiona and Chet disappeared right after her.

At the other end of the hall, Ivy gazed into a mirror on her locker door, brushing her long red hair. Madison couldn't help but stare.

Surviving *inside* school was tough enough. How was Madison supposed to deal with surviving the enemy in the middle of Jasper Woods? She slung her orange bag over one shoulder and headed home.

"Yoo-hoo, Maddie, is that you?" Mom called out.

Before Madison could answer, her pug, Phin, came running, claws clicking on the bare wood floors. He slipped and slid his way to the front door, attacking Madison with a hundred little wet doggy kisses. She wiped her face. No matter how bad things seemed at school or with friends, Phinnie could always cheer Madison up instantly.

"I'm in here, Mom," Madison said, giggling.

"Your father called. He can't have dinner tonight," Mom said as she entered the hallway. "He's sick, apparently."

Ever since the Big D—the divorce—Mom and Dad had been sharing Madison for dinners and week-ends.

"Sick? How?" Madison asked, lifting Phin up off the floor. "I just talked to him last night."

"A twenty-four-hour bug," Mom said. "How was school? Everyone ready for the trip?"

Madison shrugged. "I guess."

"You guess?" Mom said. "You don't sound so enthusiastic, honey bear."

"No, I am," Madison said. "I just don't like the idea of bunking with Poison Ivy and her drones."

"You and Ivy still haven't made up?" Mom asked.

Madison glared at Mom. "Are you kidding? Mom, we're enemies for life. Don't you know that by now?"

"Sorry," Mom said. "I can't keep track of your friends sometimes. Are you still best friends with Aimee and Fiona?"

"Of course!" Madison said.

Mom laughed. "Okay. Now, go and pack! You haven't done a thing to get ready for the trip." She

9

handed Madison a typed list. "These are the items the school recommends that you bring."

Madison scanned the sheet. Hair dryers *were* listed. Ivy had been right.

"I'll be upstairs." Madison groaned, feeling defeated. She dragged her bag behind her. Phin followed.

"Wait! I almost forgot!" Mom said. She opened up a brown paper wrapper from the kitchen countertop, and handed Madison a brand-new notebook with a fluorescent cover.

"It's orange!" Madison said, smiling. Day-Glo orange was her favorite color. "What's this?"

Mom smiled. "You won't have your laptop on the trip, but you need to keep those files up to date. So I thought . . ."

"Oh, Mom, it's perfect! Thank you!" Madison said, throwing her arms around Mom. She flipped through the notebook and ran upstairs to pack.

As Madison flung her body across her unmade bed and buried her face into a cool pillow, Phin jumped up on the bed, too, nuzzling her arm.

"Hey, Phinnie, do you want to come on the field trip?" Madison asked, grabbing his tail.

"Gggggrrrrrrrrrrroooooooo," Phin cooed, rolling over. She scratched his tummy.

Next to the bed Madison's laptop lay open in the exact same spot she'd left it the night before. She'd been chatting online with her keypal Bigwheels.

Even though Bigwheels lived across the country in Washington State, they talked online so much that it seemed like Bigwheels lived closer.

Madison logged on and found three new messages blinking inside her mailbox. She readjusted her pillows. It was easy to procrastinate. Who wanted to pack when there was e-mail to read!

FROM	SUBJECT
✉ JeffFinn	SICK
✉ Bigwheels	Read This
✉ Bigwheels	P.S.

Dad had written to explain about missing dinner. He had a fever of 102. Madison hit REPLY and sent him back a get-well-soon message. Then she clicked on Bigwheel's first e-mail.

```
From: Bigwheels
To: MadFinn
Subject: Read This
Date: Wed 23 Apr 2:42 PM
```
Maddie, really bad news. I don't have a boyfriend n e more. Reggie decided to ask someone else to the spring dance and just stopped talking 2 me. JUST STOPPED. Could u die? I am sooo bummed out. I never had a bf and now I don't again. What am I supposed 2 do? Luckily, my dad got me a kitten

today. Isn't that cool? His name
is Sparkles. But it isn't the same
as a boyfriend, u know?

Yours till the heart aches,

Victoria, aka Bigwheels

Poor Bigwheels, Madison thought.
She opened the second e-mail right away.

From: Bigwheels
To: MadFinn
Subject: P.S.
Date: Wed 23 Apr 2:45 PM
R u leaving on school trip? J/W. I
think that's what u said BWDIK.
Write back! HAGO!

Yours till the rain falls,

Victoria, aka Bigwheels

Madison hit REPLY and marked the e-mail with a
red exclamation point for URGENT.

From: MadFinn
To: Bigwheels
Subject: Re: P.S.
Date: Wed 23 Apr 5:04 PM
:-e! How could ur bf do that?
He's a dummy. I'm away until the

weekend. But I wanted to say pleez
don't be bummed. Everything will
work out, I swear. I'll write as
soon as I get back from the class
trip, ok?

Yours till the key pals,

LYL, Maddie

p.s. What does Sparkles look like?
>^,,^< Can you send fotos online?

Madison wanted to say more to cheer up
Bigwheels. But that was all she could think of writing. She still had to pack for Jasper Woods.

Chapter 2

"Madison, are you on the computer this early?" Mom yelled through the bedroom door. "You have exactly thirty minutes to get down to the car."

Luckily, Madison had successfully stuffed her duffel bag the night before. This morning was her last chance to go online before Jasper Woods. Madison eyed the digital clock on her nightstand.

6:24 A.M.

Mom's wrong. I really only have twenty-six minutes, Madison thought. But I just need to finish . . . .

She typed quickly.

Spring Fever

At 3 AM this morning I decided I don't want to go on this trip. I was imagining the bus ride there and before I knew it, my whole stomach did a flip-flop. I just know something major is going to happen there and I'm not prepared at all.

Dad's sick with a fever and that gave me this brilliant idea that maybe I should pretend to be sick, too. There are so many reasons NOT to go:

1. I have a fear of heights and falling and a bunch of other things and I don't want to climb mountains. Does that sound lame? WILL we be climbing things?
2. I don't know any camp songs because I have never been to camp.
3. We have to share a bunk and I do NOT want to get undressed in front of Ivy and her drones.
4. I can't bring this laptop.
5. I just don't want to. Isn't that a good enough reason?

Of course, staying awake thinking up excuses means that I got no sleep and I have giant black bags under my eyes, which is SO attractive. I am sure Hart will love it just like he loves everything about me. HA HA LOL.

Madison glanced at her bedroom window, which she'd cracked open. The early morning air felt warm and smelled sweet. Puffy clouds crowded the sky. Madison knew what it all meant. *Rain.*

"As if I wasn't already freaking out," she muttered to herself, "now it's going to rain, too?"

"Rowrroooooooo!" Phin howled. Sometimes when Madison talked to herself, Phinnie answered.

"MADDIE!" Mom called. "Better pack that fold-up umbrella with your clothes."

Madison searched the top shelf of her closet for the umbrella, tossed another sweatshirt and her new orange notebook into the bag, and zipped it shut.

Despite all protestations and reservations, she *was* going to Jasper Woods. She'd turned in her permission slip. Aimee and Fiona would be waiting out in front of the school.

The teachers had requested that all students "please arrive at seven sharp!" The digital clock now read 6:37 A.M. Madison quickly shut down her laptop, pulled a blue faded cardigan sweater over her overalls, and laced up her shoes.

"I'm coming!" Madison declared as she bounded into the kitchen and grabbed a piece of toast on the counter. It was smothered in purple jam. "Can I eat this?" she asked, taking a bite.

Two minutes later, they were inside the car, headed for Far Hills Junior High.

In the school parking lot, all the kids looked alike. Everyone had overnight bags and backpacks over their shoulders. Except for Ivy Daly, of course, who had one of those little suitcases with wheels.

"GOOD MORNING, CAMPERS!" Assistant Principal Mrs. Goode announced. She stood on the steps of the school, directing seventh-grade traffic. "Please enter the school and line up in groups of four inside the main gym. Walk slowly!"

Madison followed the crowd into the school lobby and downstairs to the main gym. Where were her BFFs?

"Over here, Maddie!" yelled Fiona. She stood near the back wall of the gym, under the basketball net. Aimee twirled around nearby, testing out a funky new dance move.

"Hey!" Madison cried.

"Morning, camper!" Aimee chirped sarcastically. She was imitating Mrs. Goode. Madison laughed and slung her duffel bag onto the ground. It was way bigger than Aimee's or Fiona's bags.

"What's in there?" Fiona asked. "Phin?"

"I wish." Madison smiled. "I brought all the stuff on the packing list."

"Me too," Fiona said. "It was a looooong list."

"I brought a nice outfit for the talent show, too," Aimee said. "What about you guys?"

"Talent show?" Madison asked.

"Oh yeah! I have this great new blue top," Fiona said. "With teeny beads on the neckline. That would be okay to wear, right?"

"Totally," Aimee said. "My brothers all went on this class field trip when they were in seventh grade. They said it's kind of like a party. Kids sing and dance. Like this—"

Aimee spun around for effect. Fiona giggled.

"Wait! What are you guys talking about?" Madison asked. *"What talent show?"*

Madison had packed her duffel bag with jeans and sweatshirts and clothes that she wouldn't mind getting muddy—NOT talent-show clothes.

"Since when is there a talent show?" Madison asked again. Did she have time to run home and get something nicer from her closet?

"It was on the permission slip," Fiona said. "I thought you said you read the list."

Madison collapsed onto her duffel bag, head in her hands. Seven in the morning and her nerves were jangling already? Why hadn't anyone mentioned the talent show online last night? Weren't friends supposed to tell you these things? How could she have missed something as big and important as a *talent show*? First she'd missed hair dryers, and now *this*?

Why hadn't she read the stupid permission slip more carefully?

"I wouldn't worry about it," Aimee said.

"But I have nothing to wear!" Madison yelped.

Aimee patted Madison's shoulder. "You can wear anything. You could even wear *that*."

Madison looked down at her wrinkled shirt and jeans. "Yeah, I'll win first prize in this."

"Has anyone seen Egg?" Fiona asked, distracted, eyes scanning kids inside the gymnasium.

Aimee looked around, too. "He's usually late."

"I wonder what Jasper Woods is like," Fiona said.

"Better be good. I'm missing a major dance practice because of this trip," Aimee added. "And my ballet teacher wasn't too happy."

Madison hung her head and stared at the gym floor. "I want to go home," she moaned.

"Maddie, don't stress about the talent show," Aimee said. "We are going to have the BEST time together no matter what you wear."

"Yeah," Fiona agreed.

Madison nodded. "Okay, I believe you," she said, even though she didn't believe them at all.

Teachers and chaperones rounded up the seventh graders and lined them up for the bus. Girls and guys stood together so they could pick adjacent seats.

By now, Fiona spotted Egg, so she edged closer to where he stood. Madison saw Hart too, standing there in his duck pants. He almost made her forget the talent show trauma.

"DO NOT PUSH FELLOW STUDENTS," Mrs. Goode bellowed. "NO ELBOWS ALLOWED!"

Madison chuckled. She had a picture inside her mind of Ivy Daly wedged in the bus aisle next to Madison, fighting for a seat. Madison was ready to give her one good elbow *whomp*—

"Hey, Finnster!" Hart cried. "What are you doing? You almost hit me."

"Oh," Madison said, blushing. "I was only—oh, sorry."

Everyone lined up by the side of the bus, to load luggage. The driver placed everyone's bag in a storage compartment underneath the bus. Then kids moved inside to pick seats. Egg, Chet, Dan, Drew, and Hart stood behind Madison.

"What's up?" Hart asked Madison.

"Nothing much," Madison said with a shrug. Whenever she had a major opportunity to get Hart's attention, she always ran out of things to say.

"It's supposed to rain," Hart said, eyeing the sky.

"That bites," Dan said with his mouth full of cookie. He was always eating something.

"DROP OFF YOUR BAG AND SLEEPING ROLL! KEEP THE LINE MOVING!" Mrs. Goode yelled.

Chet nudged Egg, who nudged Dan, who nudged Hart, who jokingly put his fingers on Madison's shoulders and pushed forward. Madison didn't mind the contact at all.

"Mrs. Goode is like a dictator," Aimee complained from her spot in the line ahead of Madison. "This is incredibly dumb."

Of course Madison didn't think it was dumb. Not when she was *this* close to her crush.

The line shuffled slowly inside the bus.

"There are seats here," Fiona said, picking a row in the middle of the bus. Aimee and Fiona sat on one side of the aisle, while Madison sat alone on the opposite side.

As the boys approached, she wondered if Hart would park himself right there in the empty seat next to her. . . .

But he kept right on walking. Of course.

Egg, Drew, and Chet kept walking, too.

Fiona looked as disappointed as Madison felt.

"Lindsay! Over here!" Madison exclaimed. She caught a glimpse of her other friend boarding the bus. "Sit here with me!"

As she stood up to wave to Lindsay, Madison got an elbow in the side. "OUCH!" she yelled.

Poison Ivy was standing there.

"Why don't you watch out?" Ivy hissed.

"Over here, Lindsay," Joan said, mocking Madison's voice. "Over heeeeere!"

Ivy and the drones burst into laughter.

"Why don't you shut up?" Aimee snapped, rushing to Madison's defense.

"Make me!" Joan snapped.

"Let's go," Ivy said.

"Sorry!" Joan said, not meaning it.

Madison sat back down. "Yeah. You'll be sorry," she grumbled.

The enemy pushed to the back. *Where the boys are*, Madison thought. She stared out the window and chewed on her bottom lip. She had a funny feeling about this trip. Being superstitious, Madison looked for omens everywhere. This bus overflowed with them. And they weren't so good.

Lindsay bopped down the aisle with her Hello Kitty mini-backpack and parked next to Madison.

"Hey," Madison said, relieved.

"Thanks for saving me a seat." Lindsay smiled.

"Is everyone here?" Mrs. Goode yelled.

Other teachers who were coming on the trip sat up near the front. Mrs. Wing, Ms. Quill, and Mr. Danehy were a few of the many chaperoning faculty who'd come along to supervise. Madison always thought it was funny to see teachers wearing sneakers and sweatshirts as opposed to their usual "teacher" clothes.

The driver turned on the motor to warm up the bus as Mrs. Goode read names from a clipboard. "Angelini, Todd. Armstrong, Stacey. Amman, Paul."

After roll call, the bus headed for the highway.

"Hey, Lindsay, did you know about the talent show?" Madison asked.

22

"Of course," Lindsay admitted. "I brought a dress to wear for it. If we have to sing. . . ."

"A dress?" Madison threw her arms into the air. "A *dress*?"

"Um, yeah," Lindsay said. "What's wrong with a dress?"

Madison sighed. "Everything."

Aimee and Fiona leaned over to reassure their friend.

"Quit worrying, Maddie," Fiona said.

The foursome brainstormed other outfits Madison could wear for the talent show if she decided to perform. Fiona had an extra pink top Madison could borrow. Aimee had some patchwork jeans. Lindsay even offered the dress.

The long journey to Jasper Woods went by more quickly than Madison expected. She kept turning around to see who was sitting where in the back. Poison Ivy was near Hart, but Madison tried not to let that bother her.

The farther they traveled away from Far Hills, the grayer the skies got. A light rain began to fall. Drops tapped against the bus windows.

Madison inhaled deeply and sank into the seat.

The adventure had begun.

Chapter 3

While most kids got off the bus at a rest stop to stretch out, Madison curled up in her seat and privately filled out her M.A.S.H. selections.

M.A.S.H. was a tradition among Madison and her friends. It was the perfect way to pass bus-ride time. M.A.S.H. could reveal future love and more. Madison was eager to know all about hers.

Aimee divided a blank page into columns and rows. At the top of each section were simple headings. After Madison filled it out, her BFFs would return to pick a random number. They would use that number to eliminate some responses while revealing one "true" answer for each category.

M.A.S.H.

GUY:	CAR:
1.	1.
2.	2.
3.	3.
4.	4.

LIVE IN:	HONEYMOON:
1.	1.
2.	2.
3.	3.
4.	4.

JOB:	KIDS:
1.	1.
2.	2.
3.	3.
4.	4.

M.A.S.H. stood for: MANSION, APARTMENT, SHACK, and HOUSE. This was at the top of the page.

Madison scribbled clever things into some of the spaces. She wrote down BICYCLE, JEEP, MINIVAN, and PRIVATE JET under CAR. Under LIVE IN and HONEYMOON, she included some of the coolest places she could think of, including New York, London, Australia, the jungle, and the North Pole. JOBS were computer whiz, pop diva, movie star, and famous artist. KIDS were numbers: 2, 3, 5, and 99.

Of course Madison couldn't really imagine herself having 99 kids, but she had to include at least one wacky number in the mix.

"What did you put down?" Fiona asked when she returned to the bus.

Aimee stood behind her. "Come on, Maddie, tell us," she pleaded.

"I filled out most of the columns, but I don't know who to put under GUY," Madison said.

Lindsay, who had just come aboard the bus, too, chuckled and peeked over at Madison's paper. "She wrote *Hart, Dan,* and *Egg*," Lindsay whispered.

"Lindsay!" Madison said. Luckily none of those boys had come back to the bus yet.

"Did you say Egg?" Aimee teased.

"Egg?" Fiona asked, sitting back down with a disturbed look on her face.

"I just wrote down guys we know from school," Madison said. "It doesn't mean anything."

"Then put Chet instead of Egg," Fiona said.

"Yeah, Maddie," Aimee added. "Or Joey. He picks his nose."

"Just remember, Egg is not available," Lindsay said.

Fiona gave her a teeny punch. "Don't be so loud when you say that," she said, looking embarrassed. "Someone might hear you."

"Egg is not available," Lindsay repeated, speaking barely above a whisper this time.

"Nah, Egg is FRIED!" Aimee joked.

The girls burst out laughing—even Fiona.

Meanwhile, the remaining seventh graders

began to file back onto the bus. Ivy came prancing down the aisle with her drones. She paused near Madison's seat and glared.

"Hey, Maddie, did I happen to mention that Hart and I are going to the Spring Fling?" Ivy said. The Spring Fling was a school dance coming up in a few weeks.

Madison glared right back. "No, you forgot to mention that." She knew Ivy was probably exaggerating or lying. She always tried to make Madison jealous when it came to Hart. It was bad enough having an enemy—but it was even worse when you liked the same boy.

As Poison Ivy passed, Lindsay nudged Madison.

"You have one more name to fill in," Lindsay said, pointing to the M.A.S.H. sheet.

"Your destiny awaits. . . . Let's get a move on!" Aimee said.

Madison thought for a minute and then scribbled down the fourth name of a guy for her list. She thought of writing *Drew* but put down *Roger Gillespie*, as a joke. Roger was Aimee's oldest brother.

"Get *out!*" Aimee cried when she saw the name. "Roger? That's disgusting!"

Madison laughed and filled in the rest of the page.

After selecting a random number, the girls crossed off answers until Madison's M.A.S.H. destiny was revealed. In the final tabulation, Madison was a pop diva, riding in her private jet, living in the jungle in a shack, honeymooning in the North Pole, and having 99 kids.

Yeah, right.

Her perfect guy? Egg Diaz.

Madison immediately crumpled up the paper. As usual, M.A.S.H. came out sillier than expected. Much to Fiona's dismay, everyone else discovered that she was destined to marry Egg. At least no one got Hart.

The bus pulled out of the parking lot, back onto the highway, and drove on for at least two hours more. Some kids dozed off, but Madison stayed alert throughout the ride.

"We are coming up to the Jasper Woods area in just a few moments," Mrs. Goode's voice boomed through the bus. Everyone shifted and stared out the window to see where they would be spending the next few days.

"I saw Bigfoot!" a voice from the back of the bus squealed. "Look!"

A bunch of kids bolted from one side of the bus to the other. Madison could feel the whole bus shake.

"Sit down! Sit down!" Mrs. Goode yelled. "We will be arriving momentarily. Please collect your belongings and sit . . ."

As the bus jerked forward, Madison grabbed the seat so she wouldn't crash sideways into Lindsay. From the back of the bus Ivy wailed.

"Look," a boy said, pointing out the window to a clearing with a grassy hill. "I hope we go there."

High up on the hill, Madison saw what he was pointing to: a tall tower. Lindsay said it looked rusted, but Madison thought maybe it was just painted orange. A tower in her favorite color? Was this a good omen? The tower wasn't *that* big, but it looked ominous, with its giant ladderlike steps and ropes and pulleys hanging off the sides.

As they drove ahead, a thicket of tall trees and darkness descended upon the bus. They came to a stop near a sign that welcomed visitors to the camp. Half hidden in shadows, its message was chiseled in wood.

JASPER WOODS WELCOMES YO

The *U* was hardly readable.

"Well, YO, it's about time!" someone joked from the back of the bus. "We're HERE!"

Fiona giggled. Egg had said it.

"This is fun," Aimee squealed as they stood up. "Way better than being in school."

Madison looked around. She wasn't sure yet if she liked this place.

"DON'T PUSH!" Mrs. Goode said to some kids down in front. She waved her arms frantically in front of her like windshield wipers.

As they disembarked, Madison and her friends clustered together near a tree. Camp staff carted bags up to the main lawn, where they would be retrieved later.

A short, round woman wearing a whistle and a red T-shirt with the word TRUST on it called for everyone's attention. Kids stopped chattering and looked in her direction. Everyone was handed a map of Jasper Woods. On the map, certain key places were listed and marked: Jasper Lodge, the main building; the cafeteria, otherwise known as the snack shack; a few cabins with tree names like Willow and Maple; the swimming cabana and docks on Jasper Lake; and other cabins. Madison saw a tower illustrated in the center of the map. The orange tower!

Amid the chaos of students trying to find their backpacks, several teachers tried to lead students toward the sleeping cabins to get ready for the rest of the day's activities.

"You'll find an agenda for the seventh-grade trip on your bunk," the red-shirted woman yelled over the voices of the one hundred and three seventh graders who had made the trip. She said her name was Pam.

"There's something about this place . . ." Madison said aloud.

"Huh?" Aimee asked. "What are you talking about?"

"Maddie, are you being weird again?" Fiona said. "Look at the trees and lake. Everything is perfect." Fiona spun around to catch a glimpse of Egg. The boys headed toward the Elm cabin on the other side of the woods.

"I think I like this place," Lindsay said. "Beats doing homework."

Madison shrugged. "It's too rustic for me," she said. "I miss my laptop already."

"Give me a break," Aimee cracked.

"We better get our bunks before all the good places are taken," Fiona said.

Lindsay led the way to Maple cabin, where they had been assigned bunks with at least fifteen other seventh-grade girls. Unfortunately, Ivy and the drones were assigned to the same cabin. They had gotten there before anyone else.

Poison Ivy stood in the center of the room, hands on her hips. "You snooze, you lose," she said to Madison and the other latecomers. "We have dibs on *these* beds."

Aimee rolled her eyes. "I can't believe we have rats in the cabin!" she said. "Somebody call the exterminator."

"Like, you should talk," Joan said.

"Let's unpack," Fiona said, trying to make nice.

Madison glanced around the cabin. The whole place smelled like a strange combination of mothballs, antiseptic, and burnt wood. Lindsay grabbed a single bed. Madison tossed her bag up onto an upper bunk, just to be a good sport. What was proper camp etiquette?

Graffiti covered the cabin walls. Madison silently read different words and names carved and printed on the beams overhead.

Daisy-n-Jake
2 Good 2 Be 4 Gotten!!!!
I ♥ Camp

On top of each mattress, the girls found an agenda.

Seventh Grade,
Far Hills Junior High AGENDA

Thursday, April 24

10:30 A.M.: Arrival
11 A.M.: Settle into cabins
12 P.M.: Box lunch
1 P.M.: Tour of property
3 P.M.: Talent show meeting
5 P.M.: Announcements
5:30 P.M.: Dinner
7 P.M.: Singdown & campfire
10 P.M.: Lights out!

Friday, April 25

7 A.M.: Bird walk
8 A.M.: Breakfast
9 A.M.: Activities
12 P.M.: Box lunch
1 P.M.: Talent show practice
3 P.M.: Scavenger hunt
5 P.M.: Talent show practice
6 P.M.: Dinner & cleanup
7:30 P.M.: Talent Show
10 P.M.: Lights out!

Saturday, April 26

7 A.M.: Morning hike
8 A.M.: Breakfast
9 A.M.: The Tower
12 P.M.: Arts & crafts/award lunch
1 P.M.: Lunch/awards
3 P.M.: Departure

"There is so much to do!" Madison said.

"What's a bird walk?" Rose asked.

"I'm starved. Is it time for the box lunch yet?" Joan the drone whined.

Madison noticed *The Tower* listed twice. She wondered if this meant her tall orange tower that she'd seen looming in the field.

"I heard that we have to climb to the top of the tower," Lindsay said.

"The top?" Madison's stomach flip-flopped.

"We have to fix up the trails or something, too," Rose said. "Gosh, I am so NOT in the mood for this."

"You're never in the mood," Ivy snapped jokingly. Rose stuck out her tongue.

"My brothers told me that this place is haunted." Aimee said. "One of the old cabins has a ghost."

"Ghost?" Madison said.

"I'm not afraid of this place," Ivy said with an annoyed sigh. "Are *you*?"

"There's hardly any time for talent show practice," Fiona said, looking over the agenda.

33

"Like you even have a chance of winning," Joanie said snidely from across the cabin. She said it softly, but *everyone* heard.

Ivy laughed out loud.

Aimee shot Ivy a cold look. "If we're going to be in this cabin, we might as well try to get along," she said, crossing her arms.

"I don't know what you're talking about." Ivy shrugged. "Take a chill pill."

Aimee huffed and puffed but ultimately backed down. There was no point in getting all worked up *now*. The trip was only just beginning.

Madison and Fiona decided to play Switzerland and stay out of this confrontation, too. Fiona went to the other side of the room to talk with Lindsay and another girl in the cabin, Stacey, while Madison opened her duffel and unpacked the orange notebook Mom had given her the night before.

Inside the front cover Mom had taped a photo of Phinnie. In the photo, Phin wore a glitter-green bobbler Madison had purchased for him at the mall. His little pink tongue poked out. He had that happy-dog look.

Madison smiled to herself, clicked her pen, and started in on her first "temporary" file.

FILE: Field Trip

Laptop, where are you? It's practically a washout here. Everyone's fighting and the clouds are getting darker by the minute. I bet there are huge spiders that live in this cabin, too, which freaks me out. But I won't mention that, because Fiona is scared of spiders and she'll stay up all night even more freaked out than me. And my bed stinks. I can feel all the springs in the mattress. Nightmares are practically guaranteed here.

Speaking of nightmares, Ivy Daly is up to her usual tricks. And the bus ride was bumpy, hot, and looooong. Except for M.A.S.H., of course. Unfortunately, I am not going to marry Hart. That bums me out big time. I keep thinking about poor Bigwheels and her ex-boyfriend, Reggie. Maybe they've gotten back together? Maybe not. Sometimes I feel like bad news follows ME around like a dark cloud. And what's with that tower in the middle of Jasper Woods?

Field trips are supposed to be fun. Are we having fun yet?

Chapter 4

At twelve o'clock, a loud bell sounded through the woods and a camp staffer came knocking.

"Lunches are by the main lodge, girls," he said.

Ivy poked her nose out to see who was talking.

"*That* was James," she said, walking back inside the cabin a little breathless. "And—whoa—he is a total hottie."

The drones giggled.

"Would you go out with him?" Joan asked Ivy.

"He's not really my type," Ivy replied.

Aimee hacked a cough like she would spit, which drew stares from almost everyone. Ivy looked especially grossed out.

"Got a problem?" Aimee said.

Madison held back a laugh. Aimee was fearless when it came to Ivy and the drones. She didn't even mind if she looked disgusting. Aimee would do anything to get on their nerves—and their bad side.

Madison, Fiona, Lindsay, Aimee, and Stacey strolled down to the main lodge to get their box lunches, leaving the enemy behind. On the way out, Madison heard all three enemies whispering as she shut the cabin door behind her. She wondered what made camp so different from school. As far as Madison could tell, it was the same problems and the same attitudes—just in a different locale.

The lunch box line wrapped around a table set up near the main lodge. Madison and company jumped right to the front. The boys were across the way. The area was more crowded with grown-ups, Madison noticed. Between camp staff and Far Hills faculty, the seventh graders had more than enough chaperones to go around.

"Is this supposed to be turkey?" Fiona asked when she opened her sandwich. "It looks too rubbery to be real meat."

"I know I requested a vegetarian meal," Aimee joked. "But I draw the line at rubber."

"This sandwich smells!" Chet shouted from across the way. He whipped a piece of whole wheat bread at Egg's head. The boys doubled over in hysterics.

Madison watched Hart laugh. The way his hair fell on his face made him look a little like a movie

37

star. He turned in her direction—but she managed to look away just in time.

"Incoming!" Chet screeched again as he hurled a loose piece of meat at Egg. By now, a few teachers had rushed over to survey the commotion.

"My brother is so rude," Fiona wailed, looking embarrassed.

"How about a ham-and-Egg sandwich?" Aimee whispered, poking Fiona in the ribs. "Get it?"

"Why do you guys always make fun?" Fiona frowned.

"What are you talking about, Fiona? All he ever does is make fun of us!" Aimee said.

Fiona rolled her eyes and looked at Madison. But Madison wasn't listening anymore. She opened her sandwich and took a bite. Throwing food was for boys only—at least for today.

With the help of staffers at Jasper Woods, Mrs. Goode explained the field-trip rules (because there were *always* a million rules). She also reviewed each item on the trip agenda. Madison listened closely as Mrs. Goode described the talent show. The main event would be lip-synching. The teachers had brought a carton of old CDs and a boom box. Students needed to select a song, memorize it, and work out a skit.

"So are we doing our skit together?" Fiona asked Madison and Aimee.

"Can I be in it, too?" Lindsay asked.

"Sure," Fiona said.

"Do we have to wear costumes?" Dan said. "I saw that some people have them, but I didn't bring anything."

"Don't worry so much," Madison told Dan, even though *she* was the one who'd been worrying all day.

Pam reappeared and gathered everyone into a semicircle. "Kids, we're going to split into four groups for a short tour of the woods. I will need your full cooperation along the way."

Since tour groups weren't assigned by cabin, boys and girls mingled together. Madison's group started their tour at the main lodge and then moved around the property toward the lake. The water rippled with each breeze. More rain was coming. The earth was still muddy from the bad morning weather.

As they walked along, Aimee pointed to a small clearing where she saw a row of cabins. "There it is! I swear! That one!" Aimee cried, pointing.

"What? The haunted cabin?" Fiona asked.

"What are you talking about?" Drew asked.

Aimee retold everyone the story of how her brother Dean came to the camp for a field trip when he was in seventh grade. The one cabin he'd been assigned to clean out—was *haunted*!

"He saw a ghost that screamed," Aimee said, mouth wide open like even she couldn't believe it.

"Are you kidding?" Lindsay said, half laughing. "Ghosts don't scream."

"I'm just telling you what he said. I don't know if the ghosts are still here."

"Ghosts don't just go away for no reason," Madison said. "Do they?"

"And if they left, they could come back again, right?" Dan said.

Madison eyed the haunted cabin. It looked like nothing more than a run-down shack . . .

"Boo!" Egg yelled.

Madison, Fiona, Aimee, and Lindsay all jumped like startled cats.

"Don't do that!" Madison shrieked.

Egg backed off. "Can't take a joke, huh, Maddie?" He poked her on the arm and when she grabbed his wrist, he pretended to wrestle her to the ground.

"What's going on here?" Mrs. Wing rushed over, nearly tripping on a root.

Egg and Madison broke off their mock struggle, laughing. He brushed leaves from Madison's hair.

Fiona didn't like all their playing around. She walked on ahead of the group, sulking. Aimee ran after her.

At the edge of the clearing where the cabins stood, the kids saw an awesome sight rising up through the trees like a wooden monster. It was the Tower. It stood tall with wooden beams and planks, rubber tires and ropes.

Mrs. Goode explained to everyone the Tower's history. The family who owned the camp had constructed it years before. It was a training tool like the kind army boot camps use—to test endurance, strength, and skill. And now the seventh-grade class from FHJH would be using it, too.

Madison made a mental note for her orange notebook. Rude Awakening: *Just because a field trip takes you out of school, doesn't mean you stop being tested.* She would have to write that down.

Several student groups converged under the Tower, which meant another run-in with Ivy and her drones. Everyone was telling their own scary camp stories. Dan Ginsburg said he had heard a rumor about a camp counselor who had gone crazy and started attacking all the campers—

"No-no-no-no-no!" Drew interrupted. "I heard that story too. And it wasn't a camp counselor. It was a fisherman."

"Wait a minute!" Egg said. "That's a movie. Not real life."

"Yeah, like *Friday the 13th* or something!" Hart said.

"No, it's *I Know What You Did Last Summer* . . . ," Chet corrected him.

"You guys are twisted," Dan said, laughing.

"I heard there is an old woman who has this mega-big ax and goes around chopping off people's feet," Rose Thorn said. "You're not the only one who

41

has brothers who went here before," she sneered at Aimee.

"Your brother told you *that*?" Madison asked. "What else did he say?"

Rose shrugged. "How should I know? What do I look like, an encyclopedia?"

"My older sister, Mariah, never said anything about some crazy lady with an ax. I think you're wacked, Rosie," Egg said.

"My name is Rose," she corrected him.

Ivy put her hands on her hips. "How long do we have to stand here looking up at this tower? I mean, this whole field trip is so easy. You just climb it and you're done. Big deal. I want to go home."

Madison gazed up at the ropes and pulleys. Was she the only one who was too scared to try? Was everything about this trip just beyond Madison's reach? Once a noncamper . . . always an *outsider*?

By now, it was almost two-thirty, and the students split up for the rest of the property tour. Madison's group headed to Jasper Lake. Everyone was hoping it might get warm enough to swim. Unfortunately, the water looked murky green and sludgy around the edges, not clear blue like the lakes Madison remembered where she'd been swimming before. Her Gramma Helen lived right near a lake in Illinois that was a real beach, but there was barely a patch of sand to sit on here.

"As you can see, this lake is primarily for boating

activities and summer swim classes we run off the docks," one of the camp staffers pointed out.

There was a series of connected docks at the far side of the lake inlet.

Madison leaned over and picked up a whirlybird, a sapling seed that had come flying off one of the trees. She stuck it in her pocket so she could paste it into her orange notebook. That was how she'd get through the next few days, she thought. Madison would make a collage about it.

One of the teachers blew a whistle and announced that there would be a brief snack break in the main lodge, followed by the first talent show meeting. Aimee, Fiona, and Madison walked slowly toward the lodge together.

"I feel like we're being programmed," Aimee complained. "If this is a field trip, then why aren't we in the field? We have so much on this agenda. Tours, trips . . . *towers*. We just got here and I'm already tired."

"That tower looks fun, though," Fiona said. "I love climbing things."

"I don't." Madison groaned to herself. "And what am I supposed to do for the talent show?" She was worried again.

"Relax," Aimee said. "We talked about this already. Just pick a song. We can do a song together."

"That's cool!" Fiona said. "And Lindsay, too."

"Thanks," Madison said, relieved.

Overhead, the sky still threatened rain with its thick gray cloud formations. The wind was picking up, too. Madison and her friends arrived at the lodge, grabbed cookies and orange slices, and gathered in the main room.

"We know that an overnight isn't much time to prepare for our talent show," Pam, the camp director, said. "But we do have items to help make the process a lot more fun."

The camp staff brought out boxes of assorted costumes. They kept these handy for school visitors, who almost always held talent nights during their stay at the camp.

Madison beamed. The box was filled with silly hats, boas, scarves, and more. She had been worried for nothing! Here was a costume!

Aimee found the CD for the song "That's What Friends Are For" and brought it over to Madison, Lindsay, and Fiona.

"What do you think? It's perfect!" she said. "I'm not sure how it goes, but I think we can do it. . . ."

Hart, Egg, Drew, Dan, and Chet walked over.

"Hey, Finnster!" Hart asked. "What are you guys doing for the talent show?"

Madison shrugged. "Who wants to know?"

"Maddie," Egg said, whispering. "Can you come with us for a minute?"

Madison followed Egg and the other boys across the grass near a gate. She could see out of the corner of her eye that Fiona was watching her every move.

Egg quietly asked Madison to be a part of the boys' routine.

"Me?" Madison asked. She wasn't sure if she should . . . or if she even could. "Why me?"

"Because you're my best friend who's a girl," Egg explained.

"Maybe you should ask someone else," Madison hinted. "Like Fiona?"

"No way!" Chet interrupted, shaking his head. "I will not perform with my sister."

"Come on, Maddie," Egg pleaded. "All you have to do is stand there. We'll do all the singing."

Hart insisted. "Yeah, Finnster, why don't you do it? It will be fun."

Madison felt her cheeks blush when he said that. She turned. Aimee and Fiona were walking over. They pulled Madison away from the boys.

"Enough private conversation," Aimee whispered. "What's the big secret?"

"Yeah, Maddie, what's the big secret?" Fiona said. Her arms were crossed tight.

Madison glanced back at Egg. "Nothing," she said. "Egg wanted me to do the talent show with them . . . but I said no because I'm doing it with you."

"Of course you're doing it with us," Aimee said. "What was he thinking?"

"We should practice before dinner," Fiona said, looking relieved.

Madison knew Fiona was probably wondering why Egg didn't ask *her*.

"Sorry to ditch you," Madison said as she walked back over to the boys. "But I can't do it."

"Yeah, whatever," Egg said, making a face. He turned to Chet and the other guys. "Now what do we do?"

"What about Ivy Daly?" Drew suggested.

"Yeah, we can ask Ivy," Hart said.

"She'll do anything to be the center of attention," Chet said.

"Good idea!" Egg said. "Easy come, easy go," he said to Madison.

Madison stood there, stunned. They were going to replace her with the enemy?

And just like that, the boys disappeared back across the lawn toward Ivy and the drones.

Chapter 5

FILE: Cabin Fever

Fiona is acting really strange around me and I'm not sure why. I think it has something to do with Egg. Meanwhile, Ivy is walking around the cabin right now acting like we should all kiss her feet or something. She's wearing a crop top and short shorts for her lip-synching in the talent show—I saw her practicing. She wants everyone to notice her body all the time, the way she prances around. And I think Hart does notice. Like I care. Okay, I do care.

Is every summer camp in the world like this? The bathrooms are outside, thank you very much!!! We have to walk all the way down this little hill to get there. I have already decided to stay dirty for the remainder of the trip because I am NO WAY taking a shower. It has spiderwebs as old as Gramma Helen.

Aimee says ballet camp is way different because you spend all this time in a dance studio rather than eating seeds and hiking in the woods. I wish I could e-mail Bigwheels right now and tell her what's been going on. She's been to camp and would have something to say for sure.

At least tonight we'll have a campfire and marshmallows and all the stuff I've seen and heard about camp from the movies. Lindsay told me that a singdown is when everyone joins in songs together. Sounds okay even if I don't know any of the songs.

Kkkkkkkrack!
Madison lifted her eyes from her notebook page.
"What was *that*?" she asked Aimee.
A breeze wafted through the cabin screens.

"Sounded like thunder," Stacey said, pulling on her sweatshirt. The air had gotten a lot cooler, more like March than late April.

"Guess Ivy will have to change out of those shorts," Aimee teased.

Madison giggled and shoved her notebook back into her duffel.

"Do you think it will rain out the bird walk?" Fiona asked aloud, poking her nose into one of the screens.

Lindsay looked out of the window with her. "Nah, the weather channel on my Discman radio says it's only supposed to shower after the weekend. Some storm front from Florida, I think."

"You listen to the weather?" Joan asked from across the cabin.

Lindsay nodded. "Yes," she answered meekly. "Is there something wrong with that?"

"No," Joan snapped back, gagging a little. She turned to Rose and pretended to whisper even though she knew Lindsay was still listening. "But there's something wrong with *you*," she said.

Rose, Joan, and Poison Ivy all cracked up.

"I hope it rains through the roof over her bed," Aimee said softly to Madison. "She's acting like such a you-know-what on this trip."

Madison nodded. She knew what.

"We should get down to the lakefront for dinner," Fiona said.

The girls walked arm in arm through the woods to the waterfront. Everyone was there. Picnic tables had been set up with food and paper plates and utensils. Staffers stood at three huge grills cooking up hot dogs and burgers. The entire grade was spread out as far as the eye could see.

Madison and her friends got in line for hot dogs. "This isn't very vegetarian," Aimee complained. Her parents were health food freaks and she was always on a diet of some kind, even though she was the skinniest girl in the seventh grade. She grabbed a paper plate and piled it high with tomatoes.

"Did you see Egg anywhere?" Fiona asked.

"You got me," Madison said, grabbing a paper plate of her own.

"I figured you'd know since you two are spending so much time together," Fiona said. "He's always talking to you. . . ."

Madison stopped in line. "What are you talking about, Fiona?"

Aimee twirled around, carefully holding her plate. "Let's go sit over there," she said, pointing to a giant tree trunk. "The ground looks dry."

Madison glanced over and saw a group of boys sitting there. One of the boys was Ben Buckley, Aimee's crush.

"Oh, I get it. You want to be near *him*, don't you?" Madison asked with a smile.

"Who?" Aimee said, pretending not to know

what Madison meant. But then she cracked a smile. "Yeah, I admit it. I haven't talked to Ben this whole trip. And there's space on the grass near him. Please?"

"Why don't you just go over there by yourself?" Fiona asked. She was still looking around for Egg.

"Um . . . I don't think so," Aimee said. "Why can't we go together?"

Madison stared down at the hot dog on her plate and sighed. She had been hoping to sit near Hart, of course. But now that plan was foiled.

Lucky for Madison, the seating opportunities for the evening had not ended. After dinner, camp staffers built a giant bonfire near the beach. All the kids were invited to sit nearby.

Fiona immediately made sure she got the seat next to Egg, although he was too distracted to really notice. Aimee and Ben sat together, too. Hart, Drew, and Chet were goofing around nearby.

Madison, didn't sit near Hart, however. She squished in between Dan and Lindsay.

The air smelled like smoke and Madison's eyes burned a little. But it was getting cooler outside, so the fire's heat felt good. The ground was damp, too, but she didn't mind. Madison pulled her hands up into her sleeves and squeezed her knees in front.

"Did you feel that?" Lindsay asked. She leaned over so close, she nearly toppled into Madison. "I swear I felt a raindrop."

Madison had felt it, too. But just one.

The low, steady hum of crickets was drowned out by the sound of voices echoing by the lakefront. Mrs. Goode clapped to start off the singdown.

"I'm a little hunk of tin, nobody knows where I have been. . . ." she sang loudly.

The crowd of seventh graders started to sing along with her. They reached full volume on the chorus, shaking their arms in the air and making other funny faces and hand gestures.

"Honk, honk, rattle, rattle, toot, toot, beep, beep . . ."

Madison sat there, squeezing her knees tightly. She had heard the song before, but not at camp. She definitely didn't know the gestures.

Kids yelled out the names of their other favorite camp tunes.

"'Dem Bones!'"

"'On Top of Spaghetti!'"

"'Fried Ham!'"

Aimee, Fiona, and Lindsay sang right along with everyone else. And anytime one of them glanced over at Madison, she opened her mouth to pretend like she was singing for real. Of course, "Blah, blah, blah," was what Madison was *really* singing.

Plop.

Madison felt another raindrop. A big, fat one had landed on her wrist. Obviously someone else felt the same drop, because all at once the teachers hurried together for a powwow—and decided to call off the remainder of the singdown. Everyone was ordered back to the cabins due to the weather. The breeze had picked up, too, so now the licks of flame on the bonfire seemed a little bit dangerous.

Everyone around Madison fussed and groaned at the news—but Madison breathed a sigh of relief. She thought sitting around a campfire would be different than this. This wasn't like the camp movies she'd seen. It didn't help matters that her BFFs were paired off and she wasn't.

"Where are the marshmallows?" Aimee blurted as they walked back to their cabin. "What a gyp."

When anyone spoke, whatever she said sounded ten times louder than it should thanks to the lakeside acoustics, so everyone started talking in whispers.

"What's the deal with Ben?" Fiona teased. She was in a better-than-ever mood since she'd been next to Egg for half the night.

"I don't know, Fiona," Aimee said. "How's Egg?"

Madison wished that her friends knew about Madison's mad crush on Hart so they would ask her, "How's Hart?" in that same funny, joking way.

But she kept her crush secret.

The darkness on the route back to the cabin was semi-dangerous. Fiona had a flashlight but kept aiming it up into the sky by mistake. Madison and some other classmates almost tripped over pinecones and roots. One girl nearly walked straight into a tree. Someone joked that she smelled a skunk, which sent a few hysterical girls running wildly into the woods. Of course there was no skunk. All Madison smelled was rain.

When they approached the cabin, Ivy was standing outside the door, shaking sand and pebbles out of her shoes. She winced when the flashlight shone in her eyes.

"Turn that thing off!" Ivy shrieked. She turned on her heel, flung open the door to the cabin, and let it slam before anyone else could get inside.

"She makes me want to scream!" Madison quietly confided to Lindsay.

"She makes everyone want to scream," Lindsay replied matter-of-factly.

"I wonder what the boys are doing right now?" Fiona asked.

"You mean, 'I wonder what Egg is doing,'" Aimee said.

"Well . . ." Fiona started to giggle. "Maybe . . ."
Screeeeeeeek.

The girls opened the cabin's screen door and entered the land of drones. Ivy, Rose, and Joan were sitting on the edge of their beds, unpacking items they needed to get ready for bed. Lights-out was only an hour or so away.

No sooner had Madison and her friends wandered inside than another strange voice echoed through the night air.

"Hey, girls!"

It was Mrs. Wing, who had been assigned to bunk duty. She circulated among the girls' cabins before the camp shut down for the night.

Ever since the start of seventh grade, Mrs. Wing had been Madison's favorite teacher. Seeing Mrs. Wing in the middle of this strange setting made Madison feel more comfortable.

"Just popping in before lights-out," Mrs. Wing said. "Has everyone got everything she needs?"

Kkkkkkkkrack!

All the girls—including the drones—jumped.

"I can't believe there's a storm coming!" Stacey said. She already had changed into her pajamas.

The wind was picking up. One of the shutters slammed shut.

"I think the weather is taking a turn for the worse," Mrs. Wing explained. "In case of heavy rain, someone will be along to shut the wooden shutters on the outside windows. Don't worry."

A few girls asked Mrs. Wing questions about changes in the next day's activities. The bird walk was probably going to be canceled, she said, but all events after breakfast were still a "go."

"Where do the teachers sleep?" Ivy asked.

Mrs. Wing chuckled. "On the bus," she joked. "No, there are cabins for the female and male staff. We have the same kinds of smelly mattresses and sleeping bags, too. No special privileges here."

"Yeah, sure," Joan whispered under her breath.

Madison heard her say it, but Mrs. Wing didn't.

"Remember that it gets very cool at night here, girls," Mrs. Wing said. "I know most of you have a sweater and an extra blanket, but with the rain we're getting, you may need both. Be prepared."

She walked over by Madison's bunk and looked up.

"You've got quite a perch up there, Madison," Mrs. Wing said. "Miss the computer now that you're out here in the wilderness?" She winked.

Madison smiled. "Nah. I've been keeping a notebook, though," she added, holding up her orange book.

Mrs. Wing smiled back and nodded. "I see. Well, take some notes for a write-up on the school Web site, will you? And sleep tight!"

As Mrs. Wing turned, her cotton jacket swished through the air with a tinkling noise. The bottom edge of it was sewn with little metal beads.

"Good night, campers!" Mrs. Wing called out, shutting the screen door behind her. The glare of her flashlight lit up the front stoop of the cabin.

"What is this, the Girl Scouts?" Ivy cracked as soon as Mrs. Wing had gone. "This trip is a joke."

Madison ignored Ivy's comments and opened her duffel to get ready for bed. Other girls did the same.

Plink, plink, plunk.

Raindrops hit the roof of the cabin one by one building up to a steady drumbeat.

"It's pouring," Lindsay said.

"WAIT A MINUTE!" Ivy screeched. "I have to go to the bathroom."

"So?" Aimee said. "Go!"

A few girls giggled. Ivy was not amused.

"I can't go to the bathroom in *this*," Ivy said, pointing outside. "I'll get wet."

Madison nodded. "Yes, that's what rain does, Ivy."

Almost as quickly as it started, the rain began to slow down again. The breeze was cooler now. The storm had swept through in mere minutes. Everyone in the cabin watched through the screens as the showers stopped.

Whoo, whoo.

"What was *that*?" Rose asked.

Everyone was getting jumpy.

"Is it darker out there now or is it my imagination?" Stacey asked.

"Definitely darker. Pitch-black," Aimee said. "But now that the rain has stopped, you can go to the bathroom, Ivy."

Ivy made a face. "Excuse me?"

"Yeah. Have fun," Madison said.

Ivy looked angrier than angry. Her bottom lip stuck out like she wanted to yell, but nothing came out. For the first time in a long time she was totally speechless. It was certainly the first time on the trip that something had shut her up.

Madison listened for sounds from outside. Was there a giant owl lurking out there? Had the rain really stopped? What other creatures lived outside the door of their cabin in the middle of the woods?

"I don't have to go anymore," Ivy said. "Isn't that funny?"

Aimee laughed out loud.

"Don't be rude," Joan snapped.

Aimee laughed again.

Ivy said she would rather wait until sunrise than risk walking through the dark, wet woods to use the bathroom.

"Why doesn't one of your friends just go with you?" Madison asked.

Rose and Joan looked over at Ivy and then back at Madison. This was getting interesting.

"Hey, I don't have to go," Rose said quickly.

"Me neither," Joan said.

Aimee laughed again. "This is perfect." She sat on her bed, leaned back, and crossed her ankles.

Ivy rifled through her bag, acting distracted. But everyone's eyes stayed right on her. Madison could hear the sound of heavy breathing. It was the sound of a crowd watching the enemy on the edge of . . . embarrassment.

Madison loved every moment. She knew something had to be done.

"If you really have to go, Ivy," Madison said suggestively, "don't wait. I'll go with you."

Aimee shot Madison an evil stare. Fiona even gasped a little.

"Excuse me?" Ivy said.

"Let's go," Madison said, pulling on her sneakers and grabbing her flashlight and toothbrush. She strolled over to the cabin screen door. "I'm not afraid to go, are you?"

Ivy shook her head. "Of course I'm not afraid. Duh!" She grabbed Rose's wrist. "And neither are they."

"But we don't need to go . . . We told you. . . ."

"You know what? I'm going, too," Aimee said, joining in on the fun. She leaped off the bed where she was sitting and pulled on her rain jacket.

Fiona, Lindsay, and Stacey grabbed their stuff, too.

Whoo, whoo.

"Did you hear *that*?" Ivy asked.

Madison shrugged. "An owl," she said plainly.

"Oh yeah, of course," Ivy said. "Fine. We'll go."

Madison stepped out into the damp woods first. Everyone else followed closely behind. The owl hooted again. Half the girls screamed.

"Shhhhh!" Madison cautioned. "Mrs. Wing will come back if we don't keep quiet."

"Who put you in charge?" Joan said in a gruff voice.

"OUCH!" Lindsay cried. She'd stepped on a rock.

Slowly the members of Maple cabin shuffled through wet leaves and pine needles down toward the outdoor facilities a few hundred yards away.

Madison could see the one bare lightbulb in the bathroom swinging in the wind.

"How far is it?" Aimee whispered, shivering a little.

"Yeah," Ivy barked. "How far, Maddie?"

Madison looked around. Trees groaned around them like dark monsters. She wondered how she got here—and why *she* was leading the pack.

But it was definitely too late to turn back.

Chapter 6

"Wow," Fiona said. "Look up."

The group stopped momentarily to gaze at the speckles of white and yellow in the night sky. The stars were bright, even through clouds. Madison tried to spot a constellation like the Big Dipper but couldn't find it. The moon was like a giant, white, round egg. She could even see the craters.

"Are we going or what?" Ivy said.

Another tree groaned and a few girls jumped again.

"My heart's beating a thousand beats a minute," Fiona said. "This place gives me the creeps."

"Oh no!" Aimee wailed. "Look!"

"WHAT?" someone else said with a start.

She pointed up to the light in the bathroom. The

gray paint on the ceiling had peeled half off. Bugs were everywhere—big ones, fat ones, and wormy ones. Some were dead. A dirty cobweb woven years ago from the corner of the ceiling still hung there, glued together after all this time with a thick layer of camp dirt. No one has cleaned this place in centuries, Madison thought.

"Do you guys smell that?" Aimee asked.

Madison pinched her nose. "What *is* that?"

Everyone looked at the bathroom stalls and showers. The air was musty and damp. Mosquitoes buzzed at everyone's ears. Stacey opened a stall door and bravely stepped inside.

Poison Ivy opened another stall. "It doesn't look so bad," she said, closing the door behind her. "It's fine in here. . . ."

Madison smiled at Aimee and Fiona. They loved watching the enemy squirm.

"AAAAAAAAH!" Ivy screamed. "Get it OUT!"

Rose and Joan banged on the door. "What is it? What's wrong, Ivy?"

Ivy's voice trembled. "A spider . . . It's huge. . . . Oh my . . ."

Everyone backed away.

"You guys?" Ivy's voice cracked. "Are you out there? What am I supposed to do? You guys?"

"Kill the spider," Madison said.

"No . . . I can't . . . move . . ." Ivy said. "It's near my HEAD!"

"It's okay, Ivy," Joan said. "Just open the door and we'll shoo it away. How big is it?"

Ivy sounded like she was about to faint. "BIG!"

"Open the door, Ivy," Joan said.

"Yeah, open the door," a bunch of girls echoed.

All at once, the stall door burst open and Ivy pushed out, shaking herself off and jumping up and down. She nearly knocked the flashlight right out of Madison's hands.

"Get it off me!" Ivy squealed. "GET IT OFF!"

"Shhhhh!" Madison said. "Stop screaming. Where is it?"

Joan poked her head into Ivy's stall. "It must have crawled away. It isn't here anymore."

"Is this the spider?" Stacey asked. She held open her stall door and pointed to the wall. On it, a fat brown spider measuring about half an inch crawled down a pipe. "I guess he crawled in here when Ivy screamed," she said.

Ivy shook her head. "That can't be him," she said. "He was way bigger than THAT!"

Stacey reached over and the spider walked onto her finger. "I like spiders," she said. Everyone gave her a funny look. She held it out to Ivy.

Ivy jumped backward. "Get that away from me," she howled.

"We'd better get back to bed. Lights-out was almost a half hour ago," Fiona said. "And we have to get up early tomorrow."

The group left the spider behind to eat up some of the bugs. They slipped and slid in the mud on the way back to the cabin, sidestepping fallen branches.

Once they were inside, the girls removed their muddy sneakers and wet pants, changed into their pajamas, rolled out sheets or blankets (those who had them), and unzipped their sleeping bags. Madison had brought an old, army green sleeping sack that Dad had given her when she was in third grade. She noticed that Ivy had the same one. Their dads had probably shopped together back then, back when Maddie and Ivy were still friends.

After good-nights with Aimee, Fiona, and Lindsay, Madison pulled on some wooly socks and crawled into her sleeping bag with her orange notebook and flashlight. It was a little hot under the covers. Sleepy hot.

File: Lights-out
<u>Rude Awakening:</u> Why do they call it the great outdoors? What's so great about mud and bugs? This field trip is like a head trip—especially when Ivy acts like she's queen of the wilderness.

Madison stopped writing. Her eyes were getting heavy.

She dozed off about two minutes later.

The camp staff canceled the bird walk for the next morning, just like Mrs. Wing said, so everyone woke up early, dressed, and headed directly to the snack shack for breakfast. Madison and her friends pulled on their fleece jackets. The air was nippy. The ground was still a little wet, too, from the rain the night before.

"How did you guys sleep?" Madison asked.

"My sleeping bag smells," Aimee complained. "It's Billy's and it stinks like feet. Sick, huh?"

"I kept dreaming about that spider," Fiona said, shuddering.

"That was scary," Madison said. "But the look on Ivy's face was worth it."

"I think Ivy snores," Aimee joked. "Or one of the drones does. I heard them in the middle of the night."

Fiona and Madison giggled.

Farther along the path to breakfast, they ran into the boys. Fiona lit up when she saw Egg. Everyone walked into the snack shack together.

The room was like a school cafeteria but with different decor: wood beams, screened-in windows, long wooden tables. There was no orange table like at FHJH, but the group found a place to sit. There were no chairs, either, just benches, which meant squeezing together.

Madison jockeyed for position so she'd be near

her crush. But Hart sat with Dan and Chet, not Madison. She was stuck between Aimee and Drew.

"My brother Doug was here just two years ago and he said the food is gross," Aimee said.

"Everything is gross to you," Madison teased.

On the table was a stack of bowls and little mini-boxes of cereal like Chex and Special K. There were also pitchers of orange juice and water, and assorted fresh fruit.

"What's gross about cereal?" Madison asked. "Although I wish they had Froot Loops."

"Or Teddy Grahams," Drew said, chomping on an apple.

"Well, all of that doesn't really matter anyhow," Aimee went on. "Doug and Dean both told me that the activities they have us do are really fun. It's like this total bonding experience for the seventh grade, especially climbing the Tower."

"The Tower scares me," Madison admitted.

"It's not scary! Doug says we'll all have a good time. Try it before you say anything bad," Aimee said.

"You sound like Mrs. Goode," Drew said.

"I do *not*," Aimee protested. "I'm only saying it because it's true and it's what my brothers said and they should know. I mean, what do YOU know about this place, Drew? Have you ever been here before?"

"No," Drew said simply. "I've been to camp, though, and this is just like camp everywhere. Don't you think so, Maddie?"

Madison smiled. "Sure," she said.

"But you've never been to camp, Maddie," Aimee said.

"Technically, no," Madison said. She started to explain how she *wished* she had been to camp, but then the conversation took a left turn. Drew and Aimee got into an argument about what the *K* stood for in Special K.

Madison glanced across the table at Hart, Dan, and Lindsay, who were having a three-way bubble-blowing contest in their small cups of milk. Chet looked like he was asleep; he was leaning on his hand to keep his head up. Egg and Fiona were talking. They looked like a couple, Madison thought. Or at least they looked like what Madison thought a couple should look like.

"ATTENTION!" Mrs. Goode stood up at the front of the room, coffee cup in hand. "Good morning, boys and girls. Welcome to your first morning at Jasper Lodge. How did everyone sleep?"

Half the kids cheered. The other half groaned.

Madison whirled around to find Ivy and her drones. They were sitting a table away but at the other end of the room. Ivy saw Madison look and made a sour face. She was probably still fuming about the spider-in-the-bathroom incident.

"Should we start the morning with a little stretch?" Coach Hammond asked. He was the FHJH gym teacher—but with a New Age twist. He always asked for meditation moments before practices and adopted all these funky stretching routines in gym. He wanted to bring yoga and Pilates to school.

Benches creaked and a few plates and cups were dropped as the room got to its feet. Kids grumbled as they raised their arms. Madison yawned. When she stretched, she realized that her T-shirt was on inside out.

"Anyone here know what makes a rainstorm?" Coach Hammond asked the room.

A few kids said, "Yeah!"

Aimee squealed, too. "Cool! We're gonna do a rainstorm. This is the best."

Madison had no idea what Aimee or Coach Hammond was talking about.

Coach pointed to one corner of the room and asked each kid there to rub two fingers of one hand on the palm of the other. Then he asked the members of another table to rub their palms together. He instructed Madison's group to clap two fingers on the opposite palm. Ivy's table was told to clap hands. All the teachers were in charge of foot stomping. Slowly, starting with table one, he added actions and noises until the room sounded so much like a rainstorm it felt *wet*.

Madison wondered if all campers did was learn weird songs and games and sing them before, after, and during meals. And why were they singing a song about rain when it had rained the night before?

"Very fine!" Mrs. Goode said, clapping louder than the rest. The indoor rain stopped. "That was a little reverse psychology, students. We hope our rainstorm will shoo away the real rain. We have a busy day ahead of us."

Madison looked up at the beams on the ceiling. There was a spider on one of the rafters. Its web was reflecting sunlight from the big windows.

Mrs. Goode had faculty members go around the room to split kids up for the morning's activities. The class would spend the morning helping to clean up the woods and lodge. Madison's table split right down the middle. The way it was divided, she wouldn't be on the same team as Hart, Dan, Chet, Fiona, Aimee, or Egg. She and Drew and a bunch of other seventh graders they hardly knew ended up together. Aimee and Fiona were ready to complain when Drew spoke to one teacher and asked if they could swap. He traded places with someone who didn't care whose group he joined. Madison did the same. Ivy was *not* part of either equation.

The first morning stop for Madison's group was picking up on the trails. The students were asked to clean and maintain the trails around the camp. This meant replacing rocks, picking up any litter, and other small tasks. Naturally, the ground was muddier than muddy from the night before, so the job was a messy one.

"Heads up!" Chet cried as he flicked a little mud at his sister.

She yelled back at him, tossing wet leaves at his head. She missed.

Madison, Drew, and Egg watched quietly as the mud war heated up. When Fiona got hit with a mud splot on the neck, Egg burst into laughter. Drew started snorting with laughter, too. Madison didn't want to laugh. This was her BFF, after all! But after a moment, she caught the giggles. Drew and Egg made another joke about Fiona's mud mask. Madison laughed again.

Fiona saw her. And heard her.

Madison quickly ran over to her BFF with a towel.

"I can't believe Chet threw mud at you!" Madison said with disbelief.

"Then why did you laugh?" Fiona asked. "I saw."

Madison shrugged. "What? Huh?" she stuttered.

"Weren't you laughing at *me*?" Fiona asked sweetly.

Madison felt the knot in her belly tighten. It was like a little noose around her heart. How could she have been laughing out loud at her best friend's expense? She wasn't. Was she?

"Egg wasn't laughing, was he?"

Madison's eyes bugged out wide. "Egg?" she asked, glancing back. Now Egg was distracted by the antics of Dan and Drew. "Never saw a laugh,"

70

Madison said. "He was ready to yell at your brother for starting the whole thing."

"Good," Fiona said, wiping more mud off her shirt. "Do you think I need to change my clothes?"

"How are things over here, young ladies?" the camp staff leader, James, asked. "Saw the mud. Nasty stuff."

Fiona giggled. "Yeah, well . . . that guy is my twin brother, actually."

James smiled. The one good thing about Madison's group was definitely its leader, James. He was the cute guy that Ivy couldn't stop raving about the day before. Now it was Madison, Aimee, Lindsay, and Fiona's chance to ogle.

"Um . . . should I put on a different shirt?" Fiona asked.

"Don't go changing," James said.

Fiona blushed.

"We'll get Chet back later," Madison said firmly, looking back at Egg and the rest of the boys. It had been a close call. The last thing in the world that Madison wanted to do was to alienate her BFF in any way, especially if Fiona was feeling boy-vulnerable these days.

After an hour of cleanup, the group followed James past the cabins down to a clearing, where everyone sat on stumps and rocks while he explained "survival skills for the wilderness."

"It's like that TV show!" Chet said.

"Yeah!" Hart said. "Where they eat snake brains or whatever."

"Gross me," Madison said.

"Snake brains aren't as bad as pig knuckles or live bugs," Egg said. "That stuff is nasty."

James rubbed two sticks together and a small pile of dry leaves sparked.

"Aren't you supposed to teach kids *not* to start fires?" Madison asked.

Egg elbowed Madison in the side. "Would you please shut up—I'm trying to concentrate," he said.

Madison elbowed him right back. "Yeah, right."

"What's the deal with his hair?" Dan asked. "Is it supposed to stick up like that?"

"Shhhhh!" Fiona said. "I'm trying to listen."

"Sorry," Madison said. She bit her lip so James wouldn't notice that the kids on this side of the demonstration were laughing at him.

Meanwhile, the teacher chaperone for the group, Mr. Danehy, was giving everyone the evil eye.

James continued his lecture without interruption. He showed the group how to build a shelter for rain, how to find nonpoisonous berries, and other skills. Some kids snickered, but he ignored them. Mr. Danehy kept order.

"Ivy was right," Aimee whispered to her BFFs. "This guy is way cute. Don't you think so? Maybe this trip isn't so bad."

Fiona nodded, absentmindedly. She was obviously still partial to Egg.

"He's cute," Madison also agreed. "And smart."

"Who?" Fiona said, turning to Madison.

"Who? Him," Madison said, pointing to James. "Who did you think I meant?"

Fiona shrugged and kicked dirt. "No one."

"And when you tie the knot like this . . ." James explained how to make a bowl from bark. He didn't actually make one, but he showed the group that it was possible. He claimed *anything* was possible out here in Jasper Woods.

Madison wasn't convinced.

She had started the field trip yesterday a total noncamper. She had successfully tackled the bathroom at night and located an Ivy-stalking spider. And that was a good start. But she hadn't sat near Hart once, and the Tower seemed as scary as ever.

Madison was beginning to wonder if camp just wasn't right for her, after all.

Chapter 7

After his demonstrations, James led the group on a walk along some hidden paths. Madison, Aimee, and Fiona linked arms as they walked along. It was darker here in the deep woods.

"It feels like sundown," Aimee said.

"Yeah," Fiona said. "Like nightfall or the end of the world or something."

"Very funny," Madison said, getting a little scared. "It's only eleven-thirty in the morning."

They walked up a sharp incline, and someone pointed to a run-down shack off in the distance. Madison looked up to see the haunted cabin. Then she glanced around and caught sight of the giant, looming, orange tower.

That's when she lost her balance.

Aimee tried to reach out for Madison's arm, but it was too late.

Splat!

Madison fell down the incline and got mud all over her arm and even in her hair.

"Are you all right?" Aimee asked, reaching down to help her friend.

Madison rolled onto her feet, a little dazed.

"Nice one, Finnster!" Hart said, chuckling. Madison grimaced. She could think of nothing more embarrassing than sitting there on her butt while her crush laughed his head off.

"Thanks," Madison said quietly. "I guess I'll get up now."

Still laughing, Hart extended his hand to help her.

"Don't fall again," Egg said, also extending his hand to help.

Fiona rushed in and picked off some dead leaves that were stuck to Madison's pants.

"Everything okay?" James called out. He was up ahead of the group.

"Aimee, I looked up at the haunted cabin and then I fell . . . just like that. Do you think there's a connection?" Madison asked.

"Huh? Yeah, there's a connection between not looking and falling, sure," Aimee said. "Maddie, you're so goofy."

"I am not," Madison said. "It could have been the ghost."

"Are you kidding?" Fiona asked.

"No, I'm not kidding," Madison said.

As the group walked on, Madison raced ahead to keep up with James. She left her friends a little behind.

"Is it true that the cabin we just passed is haunted?" Madison asked James.

"The run-down one? Back where you fell?" he asked. "Where did you hear that?"

"Around," Madison explained.

"Rumors," James said. "Unsubstantiated rumors."

"What does that mean?" Madison asked.

"No proof," James said.

"So you don't believe in ghosts?" Madison asked. "Don't all camp counselors have to believe in ghosts? Isn't that like a prerequisite for telling scary stories around the campfire and all that?"

James laughed. "As far as I know, the only ghosts that live around here are the ones we decorate the mess hall with on Halloween."

Madison tugged her mud-stained fleece a little tighter. It was getting a little warmer out, but she felt chilled. That ground had been cold.

"It's almost that time!" James announced as the group came into another clearing. "If you trek up this little hill, you'll find yourself back near the main lodge and the picnic table area. Your teachers have put out the box lunches. Any questions?"

"I can't believe it's already lunchtime!" Chet said. "We did a lot this morning, right?"

"I don't ever remember camp being this interesting," Egg said.

"That's because you were at computer camp, dork," Aimee said.

"Computer camp is good, though," Fiona said, sticking up for Egg.

"I went to river-raft camp with my cousin two summers ago," Drew said. "Remember when that lady fell out of the raft?"

Drew and Hart were second cousins. Hart nodded enthusiastically.

"She was so hyper," Hart said. "Camp was mad scary, though, sleeping outside in the middle of nowhere."

"At soccer camp, we mostly play soccer, but they go on camp field trips, too," Fiona said. "We went horseback riding once in California."

"I love camp," Dan said.

Madison listened, although she didn't have much to add. Her camp story was twenty-four hours old.

As they scaled the incline, the group spotted the rest of the class up by the tables, getting their lunches. Dan, whose elementary school nickname had been Pork-O, ran like a racehorse up to the tables. He was hungrier than anyone else, he said. Everyone else scuttled after him.

Madison looked down at her dirty clothes. She looked like she'd been wrestling on the ground, and she knew what Ivy would say if she saw Madison looking like this. Madison wanted to avoid that confrontation at all costs. She found Mrs. Wing and asked permission to go back to Maple cabin alone to change into another sweatshirt and jeans. Mrs. Wing agreed.

The walk to the cabin was peaceful. Madison spotted a bird poking its beak out of a knot in a tree. She guessed there must be a nest inside. A hawk made lazy circles overhead.

The cabin door squeaked loudly. It was silent inside, just the whisper of a cool breeze through the screens. The air still smelled like rain. Madison wondered if maybe there would be another storm tonight. She hoped not. The talent show was later that night and no one wanted a cancellation.

Madison changed into another pair of faded Levi's and wiped the remaining mud off the sleeves of her fleece. She looked out the window. Way off in the distance, everyone was eating their lunches. She didn't want to go back.

Why?

Madison sat down on the bottom bunk and opened up her orange notebook.

FILE: Hiding Out

We have talent show practice in a little while. I don't want to go. I would much rather hide out right here, wedged somewhere between the bed and the wall, and just wait it out until the trip is done. Someone will bring me dinner and water, right? LOL.

Me, Aimee, Lindsay, Fiona, and Stacey are singing this dumb friendship ballad and I'm so afraid everyone will laugh at us. I'm not worried about my outfit anymore—I'm worried about the actual singing. Help!

<u>Rude Awakening:</u> If I can't lip-synch, I'm SUNK.

Plus, we haven't been away from Far Hills for very long at all and I actually feel homesick. How is that possible? I miss Mom and Dad and of course Phinnie most of all.

We have to go climb this huge tower tomorrow. Now tell me what is the point in that? I'd rather fall in the mud again than

"What are *you* doing here?" a voice said. Madison nearly dropped her notebook and pen. Without even thinking, she shoved them into the bottom bunk sleeping bag. Ivy Daly was standing in the doorway of the cabin.

"You scared me," Madison said breathlessly.

"What's that?" Ivy said. "You are in big trouble."

"W-why? I didn't do anything," Madison stammered. "What are you talking about?"

"What are you doing here?" Ivy asked again.

"What are YOU doing here?" Madison asked.

"I asked you first," Ivy snapped.

"I asked permission to be here," Madison said. "So there. And you?"

"None of your business," Ivy said.

"So why am I in trouble and you're not?" Madison asked.

"Just forget it," Ivy said, reaching into her own suitcase and pulling something out. "I won't tell Mrs. Goode that I saw you."

"Is that some kind of threat?" Madison said, smoothing out the bunk where she was sitting. She slowly pulled her notebook out of the strange sleeping bag.

"Isn't that Stacey's sleeping bag?" Ivy asked. "What are you doing?"

"None of your business," Madison said.

"Well . . . I don't have to waste my time talking to you," Ivy said. Her voice was like needles. She paused to look in a small mirror on the wall and flounced her red hair. Then she continued out the screen door, running back toward the picnic area.

Poison Ivy will probably tell the drones or some-one that she found someone in the cabin, Madison thought. She knew it was time to go back and save herself any embarrassment about her disappear-ance. Madison also wanted to tell Stacey what had happened so no one would accuse her of going through someone else's stuff. Ivy was the kind of person who would accuse.

Madison plucked her duffel off the top bunk and shoved the orange notebook deep inside her folded sweatshirt. Someone would have to tear the bag apart and dump everything out to find the note-book there.

Back at lunch, Madison's friends sat clumped together in a semicircle on the grass. They were lying on their stomachs, planning the talent show "rou-tine." Aimee was choreographing. Fiona was divid-ing the song into parts.

"Maddie!" Fiona shouted. "Where were you? We've got half the song planned. You're background vocals, as requested."

For a quiet girl, Lindsay had a superstar voice. So she and Fiona had the lead singing parts. Aimee had one chorus and a dance solo.

"Wow," Madison said. "How long was I gone? You guys have done a lot of work already. Dance solo, Aimee? I'm impressed."

"You weren't gone that long," Aimee said. "But I'd been planning since last night. You know me."

Madison nodded. "Yup. So where are we supposed to practice?"

"Here," Fiona said. "Where else would we go?"

"I don't know. Maybe back to the cabin," Madison suggested.

"Ivy and her drones are going there," Fiona said. "I overheard Joan talking when she was on line for the lunch box."

"Online?" Madison said distractedly.

"Maddie!" Aimee whined. "On the line. You know what she means. Hello? We're not on the computer anymore."

"Oh," Madison said. "Yeah. Silly me. Duh."

"Du-uh-uh!" Aimee, Fiona, and Lindsay all said at the same time, which made Madison laugh.

"So where's Stacey?" Madison asked.

"She decided to sing with someone else," Lindsay said.

"Traitor," Aimee said under her breath.

"You're not even good friends with her, Aim," Madison said. "Why are you getting all annoyed?"

"Just because," Aimee said.

"Stacey just decided to sing with girls from the next cabin." Fiona said. "She said that she promised these girls before she told us that she—"

"Okay! We should get started," Aimee said abruptly. "The clock is ticking."

Madison stood up and shook her arms by her

sides like she was a rag doll. "Okay, boss lady. I'm all warmed up and ready to go."

"Very funny, Maddie," Aimee said.

"This is going to be so much fun," Fiona said.

Aimee clapped. "We are the champions, my friends. . . ." She sang lyrics to the popular song.

"We should have done *that* song," Lindsay said.

"Nah," Madison said. "This friendship one is better. Aimee's right."

Aimee held her palm to her forehead with mock sincerity. "Aw, shucks, Madison," she said. "Why are you saying that?"

"Because that's what friends are for!" Madison cried.

Everyone erupted into laughter when they heard their song title. They started dancing around.

"Hey, Maddie, what's that?" Aimee asked.

"What's what?" Madison asked. She looked down to see a long streak of mud all the way down her jeans.

"Didn't you just change clothes?" Fiona asked.

"Yeah, I must have wiped my hand on my butt or something . . . ohhhhhh," Madison stopped speaking as soon as she saw how huge the spot was.

"You should go change again," Aimee said.

"Do you have any other pants?" Lindsay asked. "You can borrow mine."

"No, no, I'm fine," Madison said. She had packed a pair of painter's pants from home. That would solve the clothing dilemma in a snap! Madison sighed and turned on one heel, heading back to the cabin once again.

Could she really be expected to take bigger risks at camp when she couldn't even keep her pants clean?

Chapter 8

FILE: Talent Show

Went back to the cabin for my pants (again) and grabbed this journal because I figured that I might have time to use it. I'm part of the backup group, so a lot of the time I'm just sitting while everyone else is rehearsing (which has officially lasted fifty-four minutes so far). This is my life on a big rock watching the time go by—la la la . . .

Bigwheels would crack up. We're jumping around out here on the lawn where anyone could see us and I bet we look really, really silly. Everyone else is practicing for the talent show inside a room somewhere with a boom box, but NO, we have to do it here with a teeny Discman. I wish I could send her an e-mail right this very minute.

Despite all the fuss, it sure is a blast singing with my BFFs. My group of friends keeps getting bigger and bigger and this doesn't even include the guys. Eat your heart out, Poison Ivy. She really does make my skin crawl. Ha!

<u>Rude Awakening:</u> Too bad they don't have a talent show for being a good friend. I know Ivy would lose that one for sure. And I would WIN.

"Maddie, we need you over here," Lindsay said. They were working out the choreographed steps for the backup singer.

Just as Madison learned her steps, Mrs. Wing approached with a stack of blue flyers. It was three o'clock: time for the scavenger hunt. The blue sheet had a neatly typed list along with instructions.

"Can't we practice just a little bit longer?" Aimee groaned. "Please?"

"There will be more time after the hunt," Mrs.

Wing explained. "For now, you have to find the items listed on this sheet. Come on, it'll be fun!"

"Let me see," Fiona said, grabbing the paper. "Wow, how are we supposed to find all of these objects in so little time?" she asked.

Madison glanced down at the blue sheet.

Jasper Woods Scavenger Hunt

Find these items before dinner tonight. Bring your loot to the main lodge when you are done. Prizes will be awarded. Good luck!

1. Blade of grass longer than index finger (for each member of hunt group)
2. Acorn cap
3. Fungi
4. White rock
5. Feather
6. Something with a pleasant smell
7. Something with a bad smell
8. Something edible (for each member of hunt group)
9. Moth or butterfly (observed)
10. Three flat stones
11. Pinecone
12. Gum wrapper or other small litter
13. Mrs. Goode's signature

"What is that last item?" Aimee demanded. "Her *signature*?"

"Thirteen things?" Madison cried. "That is so unlucky."

"I don't think it's so bad," Fiona said. "We can find all this stuff."

As Madison and her BFFs were standing there, it seemed like the entire seventh grade swooped into Jasper Woods. The scavenger hunt had begun, and kids were taking it very seriously. *Very, very* seriously.

"What are you sitting here for?" Chet screeched as he ran past with the rest of the guys. "The contest has started!"

Chet, Hart, Egg, Drew, and Dan dashed in the direction of the Tower as if they'd been shot out of a cannon.

"Hurry up, Finnster!" Hart said.

"Yeah! Move it!" Egg barked, stepping backward so he could make faces at everyone—and see their reactions.

The girls stood there gaping. Madison was surprised to hear Hart calling her nickname.

"Wait a minute. What's the prize?" Lindsay asked.

"A million dollars!" Aimee joked. "You'd think it was the way those guys are running. Whoa."

"I think we get a medal," Fiona said. "I saw Mr. Danehy and Coach Hammond unloading them at the main lodge. They're really ugly, too. They look like that chocolate candy that looks like coins, only on this rope thing. . . ."

"Should we go follow them?" Madison suggested,

clutching the list in her raised fist. "We're the last ones to start, in case you didn't notice."

"Hey!" Aimee said. "Now look who's boss lady."

Madison laughed. They gathered the things left on the grass during their short practice. Madison stuffed her notebook into her orange bag and jogged after the boys.

"I think we're lost," Aimee said. "Didn't we walk on this path already?"

Another group of excited seventh graders passed by them. One boy, Wayne, yelled out, "How many items do you have?"

"Nine," Lindsay answered.

"We have twelve and now we're going to get Mrs. Goode's signature," Wayne said.

"Let's just get the rest of the items and keep going," Madison said, glancing at her friends. They all looked defeated already.

Fiona was in charge of the list. "Well, we need Mrs. Goode's signature, as we all know, and something smelly, and a feather, and fungi."

"Fun guy?" Lindsay joked. "Like Egg?"

Aimee and Madison cracked up.

"Yeah, funny joke, Lindsay," Fiona said, smirking. "Fungi is a mushroom. Not an egg. Ha, ha."

"Here!" Aimee said, bending over. In her hand was a soft brown feather.

Madison took it from her and ran her finger along its edge. The plumes came apart a little. She shoved it into her orange bag, which served as the container for all collected items.

"Maybe we should split up to find the fungi," Fiona said. "And don't even think of making another joke—please!"

"I think we should stay together. It's getting near the end," Madison said.

Aimee and Lindsay were walking ahead, half crouched over. They found a whole bed of white mushroom caps and promptly picked a few.

"So now all we need besides that signature is something smelly," Fiona said.

The girls stood in a circle with blank looks on their faces.

"Smelly . . ." Lindsay said. "Like dog poop?"

"GROSS!" Aimee cried. She thumped Lindsay on the shoulder. "That is so disgusting."

Lindsay giggled. "Sorry."

"It has to be a bad smell. We already picked some lilac for the good smell," Madison said.

"What's bad smelly?" Lindsay asked.

Aimee jumped into the air. "Look! Egg!"

Fiona frowned. "Do you have to keep making stupid jokes—"

"No, she's right," Lindsay said, pointing. "He's coming this way with the rest of the guys."

Madison whirled around and found herself

face-to-face with the approaching Hart, who was out of breath. "Hey, Finn-ster!" he gasped.

"Hey," Madison said.

"We have an idea," Egg yelled, throwing his arms up into the air. "We have an idea! We have an idea!"

"An idea? That's a new one," Aimee said. "And what is it? You sound like a broken record."

"We've been working on this scavenger hunt just like the rest of you," Egg explained.

"But we can't find a feather," Drew admitted.

"Or a moth," Chet said. "How lame is that?"

"Lame!" Fiona groaned. "Why should we care, Chet?"

"*Because*," Egg cried, stepping onto a stump as if he were assuming a preacher pose. "We have decided that if your group and our group pool our resources, we can win this stupid scavenger hunt. WIN!"

"Even though Wayne Ennis claims he already won," Dan said.

"Okay! We can get second place, then," Egg said. "Here's the deal. We have something that no one else has: Mrs. Goode's signature."

"Huh?" Lindsay said. "I heard that she was hiding or something. So you have to find her in order to get her to sign your—"

"Nothing on the list says it has to be signed *today*," Egg said. "I happen to have her signature on an angry note she wrote home last week. I found it in my jacket."

91

"Isn't that awesome?" Hart said, grinning.

"You're a genius, Egg," Fiona said, mooning a little.

"It *is* a good idea," Madison said, considering it. "So you guys have all the other objects, including this note?"

"Except for the feather and moth, like we said," Dan said.

"And something that smells bad," Drew said. "Although Chet volunteered to donate his BO."

"Nice one!" Fiona said, pinching her nose.

"Let's do it!" Aimee shrieked. "I want to win. Let's pool our resources and do it."

The friends exchanged objects, including the infamous signed note, and stuffed the complete "set" of scavenged items into Madison's orange bag.

"It's almost time," Drew said. "We should hand in the objects, and then we have to go back to the cabins for the talent show practice."

"Wait!" Aimee said. "We don't have something that smells bad in this bag."

"Hart could just lay a big one in there," Chet said, laughing. "Hart fart!"

Everyone snickered except for Hart, who plowed his knuckled fist into Chet's left shoulder.

"This is serious," Madison said. "We need something that smells. . . . HEY! Aimee, what about your sleeping bag?"

"What about it?" Aimee asked.

"Didn't you say it reeked?" Madison asked.

"Yes," Aimee said, nodding. "But isn't that item a little big to bring? And it isn't exactly something found in nature. And what am I supposed to sleep on in the meantime?"

"Just go get it," Madison said.

Together the girls and boys walked toward Maple cabin. Aimee dashed inside to get the sleeping bag while the rest of the group waited outside.

"Nice cabin," Hart joked.

"Which cabin are you in?" Madison asked.

"Over there." He pointed toward a clearing and row of very tall evergreens. "It's exactly the same as yours only one of the screens is busted, so mosquitoes attacked us last night."

"Bummer," Fiona said.

Aimee appeared with the rolled-up sleeping bag, stink and all.

The gang headed to the main lodge to claim their prize.

Madison walked a little slower than the group. She didn't want to fall in any hidden mud puddles along the way. She'd run out of spare pants.

Hart was friendlier than friendly as they walked along. He was talking about math class a lot because he was getting a bad grade. Madison learned that he had a parrot as a pet. She wondered if that was weird. She was a dog person, but what was a bird person like? Did they make a good match? Even though M.A.S.H. had said N-O to marriage, Madison wasn't ruling out the possibility of dating.

With every step, Madison watched Hart sweep the flip of brown hair off his face. Now and again she'd catch a glimpse of his eyes looking right at her.

Madison handed the orange bag over to Egg and Drew halfway to the lodge. The bag was a bit clumsy to carry. Aimee could barely carry her sleeping bag. Was this really what camp was supposed to be?

"I wish we'd come up with something smaller that was smelly," Aimee complained.

"At least we're all here to carry the stuff together," Madison said.

Mrs. Goode wasn't there when the group showed up with the items, but Ms. Quill was. She placed the objects in a marked bag and thanked Madison and her friends.

Everyone stood around congratulating themselves for finishing the contest.

"Wait—what time is it?" Lindsay asked aloud.

"Five-oh-seven," Drew announced, proudly showing off his diver's tank watch. Drew's parents were rich, which meant he had the latest, greatest toys. "Did I tell you guys that I can play Quasar on my watch?" he added.

"What's happening at five, again?" Madison asked aloud.

"We have to practice for the talent show," Egg said, stopping short. "We should split, guys. Hart, didn't you say we'd meet up with Ivy to practice the song at five?"

Hart slapped his forehead. "Yeah!" he said. "I totally forgot."

"Ivy?" Madison said.

Although she was glad that it was her company that made Hart so forgetful, she was equally appalled that he would ditch her to go find Poison Ivy. She regretted turning down the boys' offer of singing a group song to sing with her BFFs instead.

Had she made the right decision?

"See you at dinner!" Egg cried.

"See you later, Egg," Fiona said, but he was already out of earshot.

The other boys ran off, too.

"Sometimes I feel like Egg doesn't care if I'm dead or alive," Fiona said dejectedly.

"That isn't true," Aimee said.

"I guess we should go practice," Lindsay said.

They marched off through Jasper Woods toward Maple cabin.

Almost halfway back, Madison realized that she'd left her jacket behind in the main lodge, so she turned back to retrieve it.

The sky overhead looked threatening again, which did nothing to settle Madison's escalating nerves. She was tired of rain and mud. She didn't feel like practicing for a song she couldn't sing that well, anyway.

Madison wished she could be sitting at home so she could snuggle with Phinnie. Then everything would be all right.

As she walked along, Madison spied the orange tower sticking up through the trees. In the late afternoon sun, it didn't look as ominous as it had before, but it still gave Madison hives. How would she climb to the top—in front of everyone?

Would Ivy climb to the top successfully? Madison took some comfort in the fact that whatever goes up must come down. She hoped that in Ivy's case, the coming-down part involved a hideous, loud *crash*.

Madison blinked at the Tower and tried to memorize the ropes and pulleys. She'd need the help of every haunted cabin ghost in Jasper Woods to help her climb *that* thing.

But she couldn't let the Tower distract her. That was for tomorrow.

Chapter 9

I woke up in the morning and glanced upon the wall.
The roaches and the bedbugs were having a game of ball.
The score was six to nothing! The roaches were ahead.
A bedbug hit a home run and knocked me out of bed.
Oh, it ain't gonna rain no more, it ain't gonna rain no more.
It rained this week and the week before—
it ain't gonna rain no more!

Aimee's head bobbed up and down, up and down as she sang along with the rest of the room. Everyone tried to wish away the rain—again.

Madison was amazed how many camp songs were devoted to rain.

However, the anti-rain chanting was working. Skies were cloudy, but there was no rain yet. Mrs. Goode led the room through verse seven of the song.

Madison glanced across the dinner table at Hart, who sat directly in front of her tonight. Her stomach flip-flopped, but she didn't know why. Was it nerves about the talent show, she wondered, or was it Hart's face? Madison fixated on Hart's left dimple, tracing it down his chin and back up in a circle around his lips.

Pitter-pat, pitter-pat, pitter-pat.

She'd replayed the scenario in her head a thousand times. Madison's dream kiss involved lots of rain. She imagined walking along, thinking about Hart. He takes her hand and they walk on together. As they walk along, it begins to rain, so Hart pulls Madison underneath an enormous tree. He takes Madison's face into his hands and—

"MADDIE, PASS THE KETCHUP!" Egg screamed.

Madison shot Egg a look that nearly knocked him off the bench. "What?" she snarled.

Fiona reached halfway across the table, got up, and brought the ketchup to Egg. "Here you go," she said sweetly.

Egg grabbed it and thanked her, but he hardly looked up. He was too busy eating his macaroni and cheese—with ketchup.

Fiona sat back down again without another word.

"What's with Fiona?" Aimee whispered to Madison.

Madison shrugged. "I have no clue. I think Egg is ignoring her again."

"So what?" Aimee asked. "He ignores everyone. Doesn't she know that by now?"

Madison shrugged again and picked at the little macaroni pieces on her plate. She felt like she was eating lunch at FHJH. The food tasted exactly the same and everyone had the exact same problems they had back in Far Hills.

"Hey, Maddie, are you going to eat that roll?" Dan said.

Madison passed the roll over to him. "No, but you are," she said.

Across the room, Ivy and her drones ate their dinners. Madison hadn't seen Ivy since their cabin confrontation. She wondered why Ivy hadn't blabbed to Mrs. Goode about finding Madison alone in the cabin, away from the scheduled activities. Usually Ivy would seize on any opportunity to tattle on the enemy, but not this time. Was she being *nice*—or did Ivy have other things on her mind . . . like winning the talent show—and winning Hart?

"Maddie, Aimee and I are going to run to the bathroom and go through the song one more time," Fiona said quietly. They needed to work on some last-minute dance steps they'd invented a few minutes before dinner began.

"Okay," Madison said.

Egg, Drew, Dan, Hart, and Chet were playing spitball hockey and singing at the same time. Madison and Lindsay kept score.

The camp staffers came into the snack shack carrying trays of ice cream sandwiches and Popsicles.

Egg stopped playing immediately. He had instant dessert radar—and he was UP! He grabbed Madison's arm.

"Let's go, Maddie," he said, tugging on her sleeve. "I'll get 'em for the guys and you get 'em for the girls."

"Huh?" Madison asked.

"I need to ask you something," Egg whispered. "Something serious. But I don't want *them* to hear me. Come on."

Madison was intrigued. She followed Egg over to the table where they were passing out the sweets.

"Get me one!" Drew yelled. Then everyone else yelled, too. Egg and Madison needed to get four cherry Popsicles and six chocolate ice-cream sandwiches in all.

"What is it?" Madison asked Egg as he loaded up his arms with the treats.

"Fiona," he said softly. "What's her deal?"

Madison wrinkled her brow. "What do you mean? I thought you guys were a couple."

"What does *that* mean?" Egg asked.

"A couple . . . going out . . . boyfriend and—"

"Ack! Don't say it," Egg said. "She acts like we should be attached at the hip. It weirds me out. I mean, I like her and all that, but . . ."

Madison's heart started to thump. She didn't want to hear if Egg had something bad to say. Not here, in the middle of Jasper Woods. Why was he telling her this *now*?

"I don't want to stop hanging with her," Egg said. "It's not that."

Whew.

"So what's the problem?" Madison asked. She helped carry the Popsicles and ice-cream sandwiches back to the table.

"I guess there isn't a real problem. I'm just a little . . ."

"Annoying!" Madison said, finishing his sentence for him.

Egg clicked his tongue. "Tssssssk! Forget I said anything, okay?"

"Okay," Madison said, putting her arm around his shoulders. "But please don't be a weasel."

"Weasel? Me?"

Egg leaned in and tickled Madison. She dropped her Popsicles on the floor.

"Nice one, Maddie," Egg said, bending over to help pick them up. They scooped up the cherry Pops into their arms and stood back up again, shoulder to shoulder, laughing out loud.

"Hey, there," Fiona said.

Madison's jaw dropped. Fiona was standing right there? How long had she been watching? Had she heard what they were talking about?

"You two seem to be having a fun time," Fiona said, her voice quivering a little.

Madison didn't know what to say or how to respond.

"Just hanging," Egg said. He pushed to the side and sat back near Hart and the other boys at the table.

"Yeah, Egg's a fungi," Madison finally said, recalling their joke from earlier in the day. She grinned, hoping for a grin back from Fiona.

But Fiona wasn't laughing.

"I thought you were my friend," Fiona said. She had a blank look.

"I thought so, too," Madison said, absently dropping her Popsicles on the floor again.

"Welcome to the Jasper Wood's talent show!" Mrs. Goode announced.

The room exploded with clapping and snapping. It sounded a lot like the made-up rainstorm Coach Hammond had orchestrated that morning.

The stage wasn't anything special with lights and microphones. It was just a corded-off area of the main lodge. The CD player was an oversized boom box. The rest of the kids sat on the floor in the main part of the lodge—a large, high-ceilinged room with wood beams, pillows, benches, and other nooks and crannies. It was jam-packed in there.

"We have about twenty acts, so we have to keep things rolling," Mrs. Goode said. "Let me introduce our panel of judges!"

The panel included science teacher Mr. Danehy; cybrarian (and Madison's ally) Mrs. Wing; Aimee's English teacher, Ms. Quill; and Madame La Pierre, the seventh-grade French teacher who kicked kids out of the classroom for speaking English. The four of them were seated way in the back of the room.

"Can they even hear from where they're sitting?" Lindsay asked.

"The judges are not stacked in our favor," Aimee grumbled. "Madame La Pierre hates me."

"It's okay," Madison said. "We have a great act. We'll win. Fiona has the voice and you're the dancer. We can't lose!"

Fiona rolled her eyes. "I don't feel like singing," she said. "I don't think I can do this anymore."

"What are you talking about?" Aimee said.

"Fiona?" Madison's voice trembled.

Fiona sighed. "I just don't feel like singing."

"What are we going to do if you don't sing?" Lindsay said. "I can't do this alone!"

"What is your problem?" Aimee cried.

Fiona looked away. All around them, kids were talking about their skits and routines, getting psyched for their talent performance.

"Fiona, I have never seen you like this," Aimee went on. "What's wrong? Tell me!"

"Nothing," Fiona said. "I'll sing. But I'm not happy about it, okay? *Okay?*"

Lindsay was confused. "What's up?" she asked gently. "What happened?"

Fiona looked right at Madison. "Forget it."

Madison was about to say something to Fiona when Ivy Daly strolled by. She and the drones sat right up front.

"Aren't you four wearing costumes?" Ivy asked. She was wearing a feather boa and had drawn hearts on both her cheeks. She also wore her short shorts, the same ones she'd been modeling in the cabin a day before. They must have had magnetic fields on them because all the boys were staring.

Even Hart.

"Our costumes!" Lindsay cried. "We have to get changed right away."

Aimee led the group into the opposite corner, where they each put on funny hats and pulled on T-shirts with words taped to the front. When Aimee, Fiona, and Lindsay stood in a line, their shirts read: FRIENDS ARE FOREVER. Madison stood at the end. On her T-shirt were six bold exclamation points—!!!!!!

"Ivy's costume is nothing compared to ours," Aimee said. "Ours rule."

Fiona wasn't saying much, which had Madison worried.

"Are you okay?" Madison asked her.

"Fine," Fiona said. But she crossed her arms and looked away.

The four friends in hats watched other acts go before them. Madison's classmates Montrell and Lance juggled while they sang. They called themselves Surfer Boys. Another group of girls, including Fiona's soccer pal Daisy and Stacey "the traitor" sang an old song by the Supremes called "Stop! In the Name of Love." Their group name was The Butterflies.

Fiona wasn't saying much. She was concentrating on the next act. Next up were Chet, Hart, Dan, Drew, and Egg—otherwise known as The Dudes.

The guys all had sports equipment they had found in the main lodge, and they pretended that the lacrosse sticks and baseball bats were musical instruments. Ivy played a girl in their music video, the part that Egg had originally asked Madison to play.

Aimee clenched her teeth so she wouldn't laugh. "Music video? The Dudes?" she silently mouthed the words to Madison. "Are you kidding?"

Madison shrugged. It wasn't so bad. They would definitely get points for creativity. And Ivy didn't do anything except walk around them while they sang, pretending to pose like a model. As if.

"That part was really dumb," Lindsay said afterward. "Why did Ivy even need to be up there?"

Madison shrugged. "There needs to be a girl in every boy band video," she explained. "I know how Egg's brain works."

"Sure," Fiona said, breaking her silence. "You know everything."

Aimee did a double take when Fiona said that. Fiona Waters never said bad things about anyone—let alone one of her BFFs.

"Next up, the BFFs," Mrs. Goode announced.

"That's us!" Aimee squealed, twirling around. "Hit it!"

"We have to go on," Madison said quietly.

"I know," Fiona said. "I KNOW."

Without another word, the BFFs took the stage. Everyone was hooting and clapping for them, especially the boys.

But Fiona's singing cut right through all the noise-making. Her voice was like ribbon candy, rippling and sweet. Kids sat back down just to listen to her—she sounded that good.

Madison swayed to the music in the background. Aimee twirled around the stage area.

" 'That's what friends are for,' " Fiona sang out as if she were a real-life pop singer. " 'In good times . . . in bad times . . . I'll be yours forevermore.' "

Madison hoped that what Fiona was singing in the song would be true in real life.

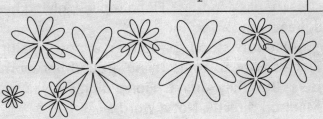

Chapter 10

Madison's eyes glazed over as she looked at the crowd. A lodge of seventh graders clapped furiously. Lindsay clapped along with them. Aimee just kept twirling. The excitement was contagious.

Fiona beamed and bowed. Then she took a second and then a third bow.

As they walked away from the performance area, Aimee whispered to Madison, "We did it!"

Madison smiled. "I knew we could."

Fiona rushed over to them and threw her arms around Aimee's neck.

"Yay!" Fiona chirped. "I am so-o-o-o glad that's over. Phew."

"Wow!" Lindsay said. "You were amazing, Aimee!"

Aimee threw her arms into the air. "Of course!"

"And you were amazing, too, Fiona!" Lindsay added.

"Thanks, Lindsay," Fiona replied, giving her a big squeeze, too.

Madison stood as still as a post, waiting for Fiona's arms to come flying around her own shoulders. But they didn't. Fiona didn't say a word to Madison directly. Not a word.

Aimee and Fiona hurried back to where they had been sitting earlier. Madison and Lindsay trailed behind.

"And next up is Sweet Stuff," Mrs. Goode bellowed.

"Stage hog is more like it," Lindsay muttered under her breath as they watched Ivy take the stage again.

Madison thought that was funny, but she didn't giggle. She was too worried about Fiona. Why had her BFF rushed away so quickly?

For this performance, Ivy wore the same costume she had worn for the song with the boys—but now she had removed her feather boa and put on platform sandals. The drones wore sandals and shorts, too.

They sang "Girls Just Wanna Have Fun" and tossed a beach ball around the stage area.

"'They just wanna, they just wanna . . .'" the

drones sang behind their leader, Poison Ivy. She was trying to dance, but her shoes kept getting in the way.

"What a clod," Aimee said.

Madison watched the enemy teetering on her platforms, taking smaller and smaller dance steps so she wouldn't fall. The room was clapping along with the song. All the boys, including Hart, were whooping at the singers.

"Whoo! Whoo!" Chet yelled.

Madison swore she saw Ivy look right at Hart. He grinned.

"We should have done a fast song like this one," Aimee said.

Madison nodded. "Maybe . . ."

"Do you think theirs is better than ours?" Lindsay asked, sounding worried.

"I like it," Fiona mused. "I think the fast ones are better. Egg's song was nice, too."

"Of course you liked *his* song!" Aimee said teasingly.

Fiona blushed.

"We'll win." Madison said. "I know we can win. Fiona—you were great." Madison smiled, hoping for some kind of a postcompliment, positive reaction from Fiona.

But all she got was a blank stare.

"Fiona, don't you think we were good?" Madison asked again.

Fiona shrugged and raised her hands in the air to

clap. She appeared preoccupied. The clapping got louder as Ivy and the drones took their bows.

"I hate to say it," Aimee whispered. "I mean, I REALLY hate to say it. But they were good."

"Yeah," Lindsay agreed, smacking her lips. "We're history."

"What is WRONG with you guys?" Madison said, raising her voice. A couple of kids nearby turned around.

"Relax, Maddie," Aimee told her.

Madison just shook her head.

After getting off the stage, Ivy walked toward them, stepping carefully in her clunky shoes. She sat down on the floor very close to where Fiona and the others sat.

"You were good," Fiona told Ivy.

Ivy ran her fingers through her red hair, which was hanging loose on her shoulders by now. "You think so?" she said.

"No, you were good." Fiona nodded. "In both songs."

"Thanks. You were good, too," Ivy said.

Ivy shot Madison a glare. Madison bristled. Was this some kind of "be nice to everyone" camp game that people played? Had her BFFs completely forgotten who was the enemy? She wanted to run.

"Hey, Finnster," Hart said.

Madison turned and nearly bonked him in the head with her arm.

"Oh!" she said, startled. "I'm sorry."

Hart smiled. He was standing so close that Madison imagined there was an electric current running between them. "Nice backup vocals," he joked.

Madison blushed. "Thanks. Nice lead vocals," she replied.

Dan came over and stood next to Madison. He made a crack about Ivy toppling over in front of everyone. Madison laughed. Egg, Chet, and Drew came over and stood next to her, too.

At least the boys aren't ignoring me like Fiona is, she thought.

She glanced over at Fiona and Ivy, still sitting near each other. But instead of looking mad, this time Madison thought Fiona looked *sad*.

There was a drumroll, and Mrs. Wing took the stage.

"We have a last-minute act," she cried. "Just in from Far Hills Junior High, a new group we call The Teachers!"

"Gee, that's original," Aimee said.

Mr. Danehy, Madame La Pierre, and a bunch of other teacher chaperones joined her.

Madison and the guys started chanting: "Tea-CHERS! Tea-CHERS!"

The music started and the cheers got even louder. The teachers sang their rendition of "Heard It Through the Grapevine." It was a huge hit. Mr. Danehy did a brief tap dance in the middle of the song, which blew everyone away. And Mrs. Wing was off-key a lot, but Madison liked that. After all, Madison couldn't really sing, either. It made her feel even more connected to her favorite teacher to know they had bad singing in common.

"Okay, kids," Mrs. Goode announced when the show was over. "Thank you all for your efforts. As a special treat, the camp staff has graciously prepared hot chocolate for us. Pick up a cup on your way out—and don't leave empty cups along the trail. You are all very talented. Thank you! Good night!"

Madison and the guys got up off the floor.

Lindsay grabbed Madison's elbow. "Hey! Are you all right, Maddie? You seem upset. Why didn't you sit with us?"

"I was, but—let's get some cocoa," Madison said. "And go back to the cabin."

"Cool," Lindsay said, walking toward the door, armed with her superbeam flashlight.

When they got outside, groups of friends gravitated toward one another. The boys took off for their cabins. Ivy disappeared ahead with her drones. Aimee, Lindsay, Madison, and Fiona walked together. With flashlights and hot chocolate cups in hand, it was harder to negotiate the roots and still-damp leaves on the ground. The air was chilly again. No one wanted more rain. But they trudged onward toward their cabin.

"I can't believe the teachers sang!" Aimee cried,

112

slurping on her cocoa. "Mr. Danehy really has the moves. I wish he were my science teacher."

"No, you don't," Madison said.

"Is that an animal?" Lindsay said, startled. She shone her light on a branch that looked a little like a skunk.

Madison looked up for a moment and saw a sky that was much clearer than the night before. "You can see twice as many stars!" she cried.

Everyone stopped. They could see constellations tonight. Madison pointed out the Archer. Lindsay spotted the Little Dipper.

"We should get going," Fiona said, checking the glow-in-the-dark dial of her watch. "Everyone else went back to their cabins already."

"It seems windy again," Aimee said. "I hope it doesn't rain more."

"Let's hurry," Lindsay said. "Fiona's right. It's creepy out here."

Branches clicked against one another. Crickets and other bugs chirped from behind bushes. The distant sound of voices from the direction of the boys' cabins echoed in Jasper Woods, even though the boys themselves couldn't be seen. Ivy and the drones weren't up ahead anymore.

"Wait!" Fiona said. "It's so dark here. Was it always this dark?"

"It's night," Aimee said.

"Are we going the right way?" Lindsay asked, waving her light.

"Of course," Aimee said, pointing. "That's the cabin over there."

Madison stopped. "Wait a second," she said. "That's not our cabin. Is it?" She whirled around and, looking up, found herself face-to-face with the outline of the Tower. It was still off in the distance, but it gave Madison the chills.

"Yes, it is," Lindsay said, clutching her chest. "Look! I see flashlights inside. Ivy and her group are probably inside playing some joke on us."

Madison and her BFFs moved quickly to the cabin. The area seemed familiar again. Lindsay's superbeam got them all the way to the screen door.

"SHHHHHHH!" Ivy whispered as they opened the door. "Get inside. Quick!"

Madison grimaced. "Is this some kind of joke, Ivy?" she said.

Aimee, Fiona, and Lindsay hustled inside.

"Why do you have the lights off?" Aimee asked.

"The lights are out," Joan said. "And we heard noises."

"What kind of noises?" Aimee asked.

"Animals," Joan said.

"Big animals," Rose whispered.

"I wish that guy James was here," Ivy crooned. "HE'D rescue us."

"Wait a minute. There's no way the lights went out," Madison said. "Did you try the switch?"

Everyone was silent.

"Switch?" Ivy said.

"What switch?" Rose asked.

"Mrs. Wing showed it to us when she was here last night. Weren't you paying attention?" Madison asked, directing her dig at Ivy, of course.

Stacey stood up and walked to the door.

"You mean the switch in here," she said, opening a small cabinet door and clicking a switch up to its on position. Lights flooded the cabin again.

"That's the one," Madison said.

Ivy rolled her eyes. "I don't think I was here when she showed us that," she explained, as if the room cared.

"We thought we were lost!" Lindsay said, collapsing onto her bed. "This camp can be a little spooky at night."

"Camps are supposed to scare you at night," Aimee said. "That's the fun part."

"I don't think being scared is always *fun*," Joan said, emphasizing the word. "But whatever . . ."

"Does anyone know scary camp stories?" Madison asked.

Everyone looked at her at the same time.

"That's so third grade, Maddie," Ivy said.

"No, it's not," Stacey said. "It's the best! Let's tell some. Come on, who knows a really scary story?"

"I *do*!" a couple of girls said.

Fiona raised her hand as if she were in a classroom. "I know a REALLY scary story."

115

Madison and Aimee looked at each other know-ingly. The three of them would always swap scary stories at sleepovers. One time, Fiona told a super-scary story when Madison and Aimee were up in her attic.

The girls gathered around a few of the beds that were positioned closest together and leaned in to lis-ten to Fiona.

"Once upon a time," she started the story, "a little kid was digging in the backyard and he found a toe."

"A *what*?" Joan said.

"Shhhhhhh!" Madison said.

"He found a *toe*," Fiona continued. "Anyway, he thought this was totally weird, so he brought it into the house to show his mom. She thought the toe looked perfectly delicious . . ."

"Gross!" Lindsay wailed.

"So she carved it up into pieces and put it in the oven for supper, and everyone was really, really hun-gry, so they ate it right up—yum."

"Fiona, that is so disgusting," Lindsay said.

"Will you be *quiet*?" Ivy said.

"*Anyway*, the boy went to bed. As he was curling up under the blankets, he heard this slow, slow breathing noise.

"'Where's my t-o-o-o-o-o-oh?' the voice said."

Madison glanced around the room. Everyone was captivated by the toe story. They sat on the edges of beds, all eyes focused on Fiona.

"The boy didn't think anything of it," Fiona continued, "so he rolled over and tried to go to sleep. But a few minutes later, the same voice came echoing through his room.

"'Where's my t-o-o-o-o-o-oh?' it cried. And the boy got out of bed wrapped in his blanket and started to walk toward where he heard the sound."

"*Wait*! Fiona, does someone die in this story?" Stacey asked.

Fiona shook her head. "No! Shhh. Listen. The boy tried getting back to sleep again, but *again* he was awoken by the strange sound.

"'Where's my t-o-o-o-o-o-oh?' it cried. The boy curled deeper into his blankets. 'Who are you?' he cried. 'What do you want?'

"'Where's my t-o-o-o-o-o-oh?' it cried again and again and again.

"'Where's my t-o-o-o-o-o-oh?' it cried. And the boy watched as slowly the door to his room opened and he heard footsteps moving toward him in the dark. The boy didn't know what to do. His body was shaking, his teeth were chattering. . . .

"'Where's my t-o-o-o-o-o-oh?' the voice said, louder and louder, closer and closer. . . .

Everyone was holding her breath.

"YOU'VE GOT IT!" Fiona screamed at Ivy.

Ivy fell right off the bed where she was sitting. The rest of the girls in the cabin gasped, catching their breath. A few laughed nervously.

117

"I can't believe you!" Rose said, helping Ivy get up again. "What are you trying to do—give us all a heart attack?"

"Isn't that the idea?" Aimee said. "They're ghost stories. Duh."

"That was a great one," Stacey said.

Tap, tap, tap, tap.

"What was that?" Lindsay asked.

Madison walked over to the windows on one side. "It's coming from outside. Maybe it's an animal?"

Scratch, scratch, scratch.

"Where's my *toe*?" Aimee joked.

Madison chuckled. "There isn't anything out there," she said.

Tap, tap, tap, tap.

"Wait a minute!" Fiona said, standing up. "That sounded like it was coming from *under* the cabin."

Everyone exchanged scared looks.

Under the cabin?

"It must be some kind of animal," Aimee said.

"Or a ghost," Madison said. "Like from the haunted cabin."

"You're just making that up," Ivy said. "There are no ghosts at the—"

BLACKOUT.

The lights went out again even though no one had gone near the little compartment where Stacey had hit the switch earlier.

"Oh, wow," someone said in the darkness. "This is so creepy."

"I'm scared," Lindsay said. "For real."

"Someone switch the lights back on," Rose said.

Scratch, scratch, scratch.

Madison froze in her footsteps. She didn't want to go back to the switch. Now that's where the noise was coming from.

Tap, tap, tap, tap.

"Stop it!" Ivy said. "Madison, what kind of a mean joke is this?"

Madison flicked on her flashlight and shone it in Ivy's face. "You're the joke, Ivy Daly," she snapped. "Why are you blaming *me*?"

Aimee was about to step in before a full-scale Madison-versus-Ivy thing broke out, but she stopped.

"Did you hear that?" Aimee asked.

No one answered.

Click, click, click.

"There! That!" Aimee cried. "Turn off your flashlights. Quick," she whispered. Slowly she moved across the room back to the screen door. Madison followed closely behind.

Tap, tap, tap, tap.

"ARRRRRRRGGHHHHHH!"

Everyone jumped and screamed and Madison thought she was going to pass out—she felt that scared. The screen door flew open with a *clack*.

119

"Hart?" Madison said.

"Hey, Finnster," Hart said with a sly smile.

Before the girls knew it, there were ten boys standing in the middle of the cabin—looking very, very pleased with themselves.

Chapter 11

"Surprise!" Egg said, flicking his flashlight under his chin like some kind of crazy monster.

Girls ducked under their blankets. Madison reached over to switch the overhead lights back on.

"No! Not the lights!" Chet goofed. "I'm melting, melting. . . ."

"That's *Wizard of Oz*. Duh," Aimee said.

"What are you guys doing here?" Fiona said, laughing at Egg. "You scared all of us."

Egg grinned. "Not bad, eh?"

"Excellent," Fiona said, appreciating the joke. Egg seemed happy with Fiona's positive response.

"Hey, Ben," Aimee said, bowing her head.

Ben Buckley stuffed his hands into his pockets

and smiled. "Hey." It was the most Madison had heard him say the whole trip that wasn't something scientific.

"You guys are *not* supposed to be here," Rose said nervously. She scrambled over to the windows.

"Who says?" Dan said. "I don't see Mrs. Goode anywhere."

Rose looked annoyed.

"What do you guys *want*?" Joan asked, flirting a little.

"Hey, Hart," Ivy said, sidling up to him. "I was so scared. Thank goodness it's just you." Madison swore she saw Ivy bat her eyelashes at him.

"But it was fun, right?" Drew asked.

"Excuse me? Was I talking to you?" Ivy said.

"What were you guys doing in here besides talking about us—ha, ha, ha," Chet said, snapping his fingers.

Madison chuckled. "Hanging out telling stories. Ghost stories," she said.

"Perfect!" Egg said. "So we came in right on cue."

"Actually," Madison said, seizing the moment, "Fiona was telling the story. You would have loved it, Egg."

Fiona gave Madison a quizzical look.

"I think Fiona is maybe the best ghost-story teller I've ever heard," Madison went on. "Don't you think so, Aim?"

"I was definitely spooked," Aimee said. She smiled at Ben again.

Most of the girls in the room were giggling by now, avoiding looks from boys they didn't like and staring at boys they did. Stacey the quiet girl sat back down on her bed and nervously pulled all the blankets up around her. Joan started telling all the boys what to do. Lindsay and Dan were counting the moths on the screens.

Of course Fiona was beaming at Egg. And for the first time on the field trip, Egg was beaming back.

"What were all those noises you guys were making?" Madison asked.

"Noises? Huh?" Egg asked. "We were just hanging outside, waiting until the right moment. We didn't make any noises. . . ."

"Not deliberately," Drew said.

"Booooooooooo!" Chet cried, cracking himself up. "Noises like that?"

The girls exchanged glances, eyebrows raised.

"No, dork," Fiona cut in. "Like 'scratch, scratch.'"

"And 'tap, tap, tap,'" Madison said.

"What are you talking about?" Hart asked. "Egg isn't joking around. We really were trying to be *quiet*, not make noises."

The room got totally silent.

"If you guys are lying to us, I swear . . ." Ivy said.

"Take a chill pill, girlfriend," Chet said.

Drew laughed so hard, he snorted.

"Seriously," Madison said. "Ivy's right. If you guys didn't make the noises then it must be the ghosts. From the haunted cabin."

"Haunted what?" Dan said.

"I know," Egg replied. "Mariah told me about the haunted cabin here. When her class took its field trip a couple of years ago, they heard all these strange noises in the middle of the night, and the lights kept going out. . . ."

"Are you kidding?" Lindsay said. She looked over at Madison.

"The lights went out here tonight," Madison said aloud.

"Yeah, but it wasn't a ghost," Egg said. "Come on, Maddie, do you believe in ghosts? Do any of you really believe in ghosts?"

Every girl in the room nodded emphatically.

"It's unanimous," Madison said. "We all believe in ghosts." Even Ivy and the drones believed.

"Me too," Drew said. "I believe."

"And me," Hart said. "Why not? Ghosts are cool."

Scratch, scratch, scratch.

"There!" Ivy shrieked. "Did you hear that?"

The room hushed.

Scratch, scratch, scratch.

"OH MY GOD!" Aimee screamed.

"Shhhhhhh!" one of the boys said. "Mrs. Goode will hear you."

"Sorry," Aimee said.

"Is that the noise you heard before?" Egg asked the room.

Everyone nodded.

"You should go outside and see what it is," Lindsay said.

"Not me," Egg said, laughing. "I'm not going to get eaten by some monster who lives in Jasper Woods."

"Don't say that," Stacey said meekly. She looked like she wanted to cry. Some other girls and boys were feeling extra nervous all of a sudden.

"You really should turn the lights out," Hart suggested. "So someone doesn't see us all in here."

"Not with a ghost on the loose," Fiona said, giggling.

Egg giggled, too. "Yeah. What she said."

"I think the noise is coming from the haunted cabin," Madison said.

"Well, you would think that, wouldn't you?" Joan the drone said. She turned to a cute boy from Egg's cabin. "Don't you think we should just stay here and stop talking about ghosts? I do."

Madison heard another scratching noise, only this one sounded like it was closer than the ghost cabin, on the perimeter of their own.

"We have to go and investigate," Madison suggested. She looked over at Hart and bravely said, "Will you come with me?"

Hart's jaw slackened. His eyes bugged out.

Madison was sure he would say no. And then he smiled.

"Totally," Hart said.

"I'll go, too," Dan said. "I don't believe in haunted cabins, but I'll go."

None of the other girls wanted to come along.

"I'll watch from here."

"I'm allergic to ghosts."

"I don't want to get caught by Mrs. Goode."

Apparently the assistant principal was more threatening and scary than the haunted cabin.

Madison gulped as she headed for the darkness outside.

Ivy grabbed her arm. "You don't have to be such a show-off, Maddie. You look really dumb, you know," Ivy whispered.

Madison turned to face the enemy. "I don't care," she said calmly, and pushed open the cabin's screen door.

"Go, Maddie!" Lindsay cheered.

Aimee took Madison by the shoulders. "What if there really is a ghost?" she asked with mock seriousness. Then she burst into a horsey laugh. "HA! HA!"

Joan and Rose laughed nervously. Madison took note since the drones were so rarely speechless.

Chet hooted. "Go, Ghostbusters!"

Fiona cringed. "That is the dumbest thing I have ever heard," she said. "Why aren't you going out there, brother?"

Chet made a face. "I like it in here," he said, wearing an evil grin. He was still busy checking out the seventh-grade girls.

"Well, I won't miss out on the fun," Egg called out, following Hart, Dan, and Madison out of the cabin. Fiona went out the door right after him.

The air outside was thick with weird fog.

"This wasn't here when we came by a little while ago," Hart said. He was following Madison and the superbeam Lindsay had loaned her.

There was always pea-soup fog in horror movies like *The Werewolf*, Madison thought.

Madison had to admit to herself that she was a little scared. Every little thing that went bump in the night sent a giant shiver down her spine.

And it got worse.

No sooner had Madison, Hart, and the rest of the small group been outside together than raindrops started to fall, slowly at first. But then they were falling more steadily. Egg stood in one place and stuck out his tongue, like he was getting a personal drink from the skies.

And it got worse.

Madison heard the scratching noise again. She wandered around the cabin with the flashlight shining, but it started to blink a little. And then it went out completely. Dan yanked his flashlight out of his pocket and loaned it to her.

"Let there be light," Madison joked.

127

The first person she saw in the new yellow light was Hart. He smoothed back his wet hair. The rain was starting to fall even harder.

"Hey!" a voice yelled out in a loud whisper from the cabin windows. "What are you guys doing?"

Madison shone the high beam into the cabin. Everyone ducked.

"Force of habit," Aimee said afterward, standing back up.

The rain felt warm on Madison's forehead. Her raincoat wasn't doing its water-repellent thing, but she plodded onward. Hart was right behind her, like in her dream fantasy sequence, only better. All Madison needed was the kiss under the tree—and an eraser to make all these other people go away.

Egg, Dan, and Fiona were right behind them. Madison could hear them whispering.

"You really think our surprise was fun?" Egg asked Fiona.

Fiona sounded like she'd been practicing this for weeks. "You know how I feel, Egg," she said.

Dan groaned. "Quit getting all sappy," he said. "You guys are so weird."

Madison wanted to turn and jump into the air in a half-split "hoorah!" over the reconciliation of Egg and Fiona but (a) she didn't know how to do any kind of split, especially not in the rain, and (b) she didn't want to jeopardize things between herself and her BFF any more than she already had.

"Okay, my feet are soaked. I'm going back," Egg said abruptly.

Dan agreed. "Yeah, it's wet," he said. "Besides, I don't want to get caught. The teacher cabin is just over there."

"It is?" Madison asked. She glanced over at it. Half the lights were on.

"We should go back," Fiona said. "Maybe the ghosts have gone to sleep."

"Very funny," Madison said.

The boys turned to walk away—even Hart.

"I think we're rained out," he said.

"Are you all leaving me here?" Madison asked.

In the half darkness, Fiona made her way to Madison's side. "Do you want me to go all the way to the haunted cabin with you? We can do it together. . . ."

"What!" Madison said. "Is this some kind of trick? An hour ago you didn't even look me in the eye. And you were talking to Ivy!"

By now, the boys had wandered out of earshot, back to their cabin.

"I know," Fiona said. "I was doing that to make you mad. I was mad."

"Wow," Madison said. "I was so worried."

"I was mad about Egg before, but I'm not anymore."

"Huh?" Madison asked. "Why were you mad about Egg?"

"I'm not sure. But now it's over and I want my friend back," Fiona said."

An owl whoo-whooed, and Madison nearly leaped out of her skin.

"Let's get back," Madison said. "This is creepier than creepy."

Fiona grabbed Madison's arm and squeezed so she wouldn't fall down. But Madison knew what was really going on. That squeeze meant "I'm sorry" in BFF body language.

"I'm so glad we made up," Fiona said.

Madison sighed. "Not as glad as me."

Chapter 12

FILE: Ghosts

This field trip has been SUCH an eye-opener. I thought that I would be in the dark about so many things—and the truth is that I am just as brave as anyone who's been going to camp for a million years. Turns out that the mysterious noises last night were birds on the roof of the cabin, BTW. We saw them there this morning, nesting. They must have been rebuilding because of all the rain. Go figure.

Right now I am sitting on the cabin

steps, looking out at the pine trees around us. They look a lot less scary in daytime. We made it all the way to the haunted cabin last night and were looking around for ghosts, but then Fiona got tired, so we left.

I wish I had my Ouija board or even just my Magic 8-Ball. Something to help me find out for real if there are ghosts here or not. I feel like there must be. I just have this ghost vibe. Can't wait to write Bigwheels all about this. She'd probably say I should go ask the blowfish on bigfishbowl.com. But I can't do that here, either. No online hookups in the middle of the woods—although there may be some other kinds of hookups, LOL!

I still miss my laptop sooo much.

"Maddie!" Fiona called out.

"There you are!" Aimee said. Their voices echoed. The stillness of the early morning air amplified every noise and motion as if the volume had been turned way up.

Madison closed her orange notebook, leaving the pen inside to mark her place.

"Good morning," Madison said.

Fiona and Aimee sat on either side of Madison, making a BFF sandwich. They squeezed hard.

"I'm so glad you and Fiona are talking again," Aimee said with a sigh.

"I hate fighting," Madison said. "Even though what happened wasn't really classified as a fight, I hated it."

Fiona nodded. "Me too."

"It's warm today," Aimee said, tugging off her fleece.

"Should we go to breakfast?" Fiona asked. She stood up and brushed off her pants. "We find out who won the talent show today. I can't wait! I thought about it all last night. After the guys, of course."

Aimee giggled. "What else is on our schedule?"

"Well, we have to pack," Madison said. "Since we're going home. It seems like we just got here."

"Home? I'm not ready to go home until we have our award luncheon," Fiona said, smiling. "We won something. I can feel it!"

"Everyone wins something," Aimee said. "That's how camp works. No one feels left out."

"Don't forget the Tower climb," Fiona said.

Madison lowered her head. The Tower? With all the other excitement, she had nearly forgotten. Madison had a vision of herself swinging from ropes and vines like Tarzan, slamming into the side of the Tower with a bone-breaking thud.

That would make for a good photo on the school Web site.

"Maddie, what's wrong? Aren't you psyched for the Tower?" Aimee asked.

Madison flashed a grin. "Sure, I am," she said, not believing a word.

As they walked to breakfast, they caught up with the boys, just as they had the morning before. Ben was with the boy group today, and Aimee wasted no time getting closer to him. He talked about sunlight, the properties of mud, and the direction of the wind. Not exactly romantic stuff, Madison thought, but Aimee looked smitten. Once again, Fiona and Egg walked as an item, too. It almost looked like they were touching hands.

Watching her friends paired off with boys was difficult for Madison, but she shrugged it off. She loped toward Hart, hoping he'd get in step with her, but that didn't work. Hart walked ahead with Chet and Drew instead. Dan came up to Madison and gave her a little shove.

"Why so glum, chum?" Dan asked. "Hungry?"

Madison laughed. "Not really. But I'd be willing to guess that you are."

Now Dan laughed. "Yeah, but I'm sick of this camp food. I'm ready to go home."

"Me too," Madison said. "And I don't want to climb that Tower."

"Me neither," Dan admitted.

Madison was relieved that someone else was nervous about scaling the wooden monster. The two vowed to cheer each other on once the climbing started.

Inside the snack shack, the camp staffers had made a special breakfast for day three of the Jasper Woods field trip: hotcakes. Trays of silver-dollar cakes filled a long table that also held buckets of syrup, sliced bananas, berries, and crisp bacon.

Dan licked his lips. "Now, *this* is better than cereal," he cried, getting on line for his own plate piled high with food.

"Hey, Finnster," Hart said, finally acknowledging Madison on the breakfast line. "Way to go last night."

"Yeah, Maddie," Egg joined in. "You're like the scare patrol or something."

"Shh . . . don't tell anyone," Madison said. "If the teachers found out—"

"Your secret is safe . . ." Hart said. The corners of his mouth turned up. His hair was doing that cute "flop" thing over his brow.

Madison fiddled nervously with the tablecloth on the serving table. Without realizing it, she knocked over a bowl filled with little plastic containers of butter. They hit the floor and scattered.

"Here, let me help," Hart said, bending over.

Madison got down to retrieve them, too. She was practically nose-to-nose with Hart.

"Thanks," Madison mumbled, embarrassed.

"HART!" Ivy's voice pierced the air. She continued to whine over Madison's head. "Hart, I was looking for you. We saved you a seat over here. Come on. Come *on*!"

Hart glanced at Madison and stood up. He dumped the butters in his hand back into the bowl. "See ya," Hart said, turning toward Ivy.

"Yeah," Madison said. "See ya."

By now Aimee, Ben, Fiona, and Egg were all on bended knee, helping Madison pick up the mess. Madison watched Hart follow Ivy over to a table with the drones. Ivy glanced back, snickering. She always gets what she wants: Madison thought—especially when it comes to guys.

As she looked down, Madison realized that her jeans were now dirty from the floor where she'd been kneeling. "Great," Madison said aloud to herself. "Not only do I feel bad. Now I look bad."

Madison's bad luck with pants continued.

Mrs. Goode called the room to attention to announce the morning plans. But Madison wasn't really listening that well. She couldn't take her eyes off Hart and Ivy. Many of the kids were sitting in different seats than the day before. Cliques were mixed together now.

It was every camper for himself or herself.

"Before we get started," Mrs. Goode said, "we have some business to attend to. Last night there were some reports of students in the woods after lights-out . . . reports that I am hesitant to acknowledge. . . ."

Chet giggled, and Mrs. Goode looked over at him quizzically.

"Something you wish to share, Mr. Waters?" she asked. He shook his head rapidly.

Aimee gave Madison a thumbs-up. Luckily, none of the boys or girls who had been at the ghost hunt would talk. This was one secret the seventh-grade boys and girls could share together—even Poison Ivy would keep a lid on it.

Mrs. Goode eyed the crowd as if some additional clues might mysteriously drop from the rafters or glow on kids' foreheads—but none did.

"Lucky for everyone involved, the night stroll happened without incident," Mrs. Goode continued. "And we will leave the matter at that. Am I understood?"

Aimee sat next to Madison on a snack shack bench. On the other side of Aimee, Ben explained how with one tiny *flick*, he could send a forkful of pancakes toward Mrs. Goode's head at a 180-degree trajectory. Madison wanted to laugh—he sounded like such a smarty know-it-all. But Aimee looked genuinely happy to be sitting near him, listening to all he had to say.

After stuffing themselves, the kids lined up for the morning hike to the Tower. Everyone had on sneakers for climbing. Madison noticed Ivy was wearing a cool pair of blue ones with a white stripe that Madison had seen in the Boop-Dee-Doop catalog. Even at camp, Ivy always made a fashion statement.

After leaving breakfast, all 103 seventh graders marched across the lawn, into the woods, and over to the giant Tower. The sky had gotten cloudy all over again, and a light mist was falling. Madison hoped it would rain now because that meant no climbing.

But she had no luck in that department. The rain was only a sprinkle. The climb was on.

The Tower itself was nearly sixty feet high. Beneath it, camp staffers waited along with FHJH faculty members, each holding many-colored flags. Off to the left was an elaborate obstacle course with cones and ropes and pits filled with mud. There was mud to spare at this camp.

Kids were divided into blue, green, red, orange, and yellow teams of about twenty. Madison crossed her fingers so she'd get into the orange group. Unfortunately, she was put into green. But Lindsay was orange, so they switched. At least I have my favorite color going for me, Madison thought.

Pam, the camp director, explained that the groups would spend the majority of time getting kids up and down the Tower. In the meantime, those not climbing would run the obstacle course. Each student was timed for speed through the course. Best time meant a prize that day at lunch.

Madison leaned back and arched her neck to see what she was up against. Every level had wide beams and rope steps. Pam said there were twenty different ways to get up to the top. The camp staffers handed out helmets and harnesses to the first kids who wanted to climb. Madison was not among the first crop of climbers. She, along with everyone else, watched the adventure unfold on the ground.

Hart pulled on his helmet before anyone else. He bragged that he'd climbed a forty-foot tower once before, at a wilderness camp he visited two summers earlier. Madison swooned at the sight of him in his gear. He waved to the rest of the seventh grade and began his ascent.

"Go, Hart," Drew said.

"Yay!" Madison said, cheering him on.

Everyone around them was clapping. Ivy had her hands high in the air. "You can do it!" Ivy shrieked so loud, kids plugged their ears.

After Hart, Egg, Chet, and Drew grabbed the ropes and shimmied, lifted, and climbed their way to the top. Dozens of kids jumped to the front of the line and celebrated their climbs.

But Madison was the leader for a group of "I can't do it" seventh graders. Some felt self-conscious about the way they looked. Others had a fear of heights. Others felt too weak. Members included Ivy Daly, Rose Thorn, and Phony Joanie, whose brazen excuse was, "This tower is stupid." Since the activity wasn't for a grade or merit, no drone saw the point in climbing. As each girl was called for her "turn," they each found some excuse.

"I don't want to hurt myself," Ivy told the camp staffer who was trying to get her into a harness to climb. "And I don't want to break one of my nails. That would be even worse."

Madison knew Ivy just wanted to hang out around James, the cute staff counselor, who was supervising the obstacle course.

"Ms. Finn." Pam was reading from a list of names. "Can we get your gear on for the climb?"

Madison felt woozy. She was as scared as she'd been all morning.

"Um . . ."

Her throat felt parched. All around her was a hum of kids with climbing gear and fall leaves and . . .

"Okay," Madison said, leaving her fear in the dirt and approaching the helmets. "Can I wear the orange helmet?" she asked.

Pam nodded. "Go right ahead," she told Madison, winking.

Madison knew Mom and Dad would be proud of her accomplishments in forty-eight short hours. But it was Hart who Madison really wanted to impress. Had he finished his obstacle course yet? She almost wanted to climb aboard the Tower and scream, "HEY, HART! LOOK OVER HERE!"

The air still felt damp, but it didn't make the Tower slippery, so the climbing continued. Madison's climb was all systems *go*. Another six kids from class ascended at the same time. One of the climbers in Madison's little group fell backward but dangled in his harness. Those watching from below gasped. The camp staffers waved. "It's okay! Everyone's okay!"

Madison climbed on. She put one foot at a time into rope ladder segments, onto blocks, and on top of large rough-hewn beams. If she was going to do this, then *she was going to do this*.

She caught her breath on beam number five (she was counting) and pulled herself up on a rope. Her helmet squeezed hot on her head. All she could think was, Boy, am I going to have a bad hair afternoon, and, Please don't let me fall off this next beam, as she groped and grabbed her way up the structure. The cheers from below continued, but Madison couldn't tell if they were for her, for another kid on the Tower, or for the large percentage of classmates who were navigating the obstacle course.

She climbed on.

About ten feet from the top of the Tower, Madison felt a pang of fear. Her fingers ached a little. She wanted to quit. She wanted to let go and fall in that harness. But she did none of those things.

She climbed on.

"Go, Maddie!" Fiona and Aimee were squealing as loudly as they could from the bottom of the Tower. They had both made it to the top already. Madison aimed for clouds.

Madison grabbed at a large, dangling, knotted rope at the very top part of the Tower, but she couldn't quite reach it. She rested for a deep breath, just a second. Then she moved on again.

She held on to a wooden ring and then a rope pulley, edging slowly upward. Her helmet itched. One step she took missed, but she didn't come rappelling off the tower. She grabbed another wooden grip in time to save herself from dropping off. Whew. Her arms felt like noodles.

Up high, there in the sky, the air was chillier than down below. Air was damp from all the rain the sky had been delivering for the past few days. Madison gazed at where the sun should have been shining. It looked more like a white-gray glow from behind clouds. But in the middle of all that rainy sky, in a small patch of azure sky no bigger than a football field, Madison saw something that was most definitely not bad weather.

Madison saw a rainbow.

"Look at that!" she cried. No one down below heard her, but it didn't matter. The rainbow's arrival was perfectly timed. This was the sign she'd been waiting for the entire field trip. The sign that proved she could do it.

Clap, clap, clap, clap, clap.

Madison reeled as she leaned over one rope to see where the noise was coming from. Down below, the seventh graders from the obstacle course had gathered anew under the Tower. Everyone was clapping. Was their applause for the rainbow? Or was it for Madison?

"Go, Ivy!" Hart cried. Madison heard his voice above all the others.

Go, Ivy?

Madison felt a knot in her throat. Her foot slipped a little, and she wondered if she should just give up and let go. What was the point of continuing when the only person Hart ever noticed was Poison Ivy?

But Madison stayed focused. She pulled herself up onto the very last beam. Taking a deep, cool breath, she sat on the top of the Tower and gazed up into the rainbow.

You can go, Ivy, Madison thought. Go *away*. I'm the new queen of the wilderness.

Chapter 13

Sunlight poured in through the cabin's screened-in windows. Madison couldn't help but laugh. The trip was over—and *now* the weather was nice?

She scratched her head and contemplated taking a shower before heading home but decided against it. Going to the bathroom outside the cabin had been hard enough. She didn't feel like getting wet and cold with pine needles between her toes *now*. And who took a camp shower in the middle of the day? Instead, she changed out of the clothes she'd been wearing on the Tower. Madison pulled on her last clean orange T-shirt, cargo capri pants she borrowed from Fiona, and sneakers. After packing up everything else, she disappeared outside for a few moments to write in her orange notebook.

FILE: The Tower

I saw the world differently from up on the Tower. I was a little closer to the sky and trees. Why did the air feel different up there? I looked across a clearing in the woods and saw the different cabins from above.

I could see my friends, waving up at me, looking up to me. Me!

<u>Rude Awakening:</u> Usually when people act all high and mighty, it bugs me. But today, when I was standing on the Tower, I felt high and mighty. And it was very cool.

Why was I so scared about camp? I can't even remember.

Madison took a deep breath, picked up her notebook, and walked back into the cabin. Some other girls had changed their outfits for lunch and the bus ride home.

"Didn't you have fun this morning?" Lindsay asked Madison, struggling to squeeze her clothes into a bag that was too small for everything. "That was such a rush."

"Yeah," Madison said, smiling to herself. "I'm almost sad to leave camp."

"Don't get carried away," Aimee called from the other side of the room. She walked over to Madison.

"I mean, do you want to stay here another night? Be honest."

"I do!" Fiona said, smiling. She lugged her bag to the screen door and pushed it outside.

"What's she so happy about?" Poison Ivy grumbled.

"You did it, Maddie," Aimee said, wrapping her arm around Madison's shoulders. "You made it through camp."

"Well, it's not really camp," Madison said. "I mean, it's not like I've been here for weeks and weeks."

"You gotta start somewhere!" Lindsay said.

Fiona poked her head back into the cabin. "Hurry up, everyone," she said. "I see some people heading down to the main lodge already."

"We still have time," Joan the drone barked. She was folding all of her clothes into perfect squares.

"What's your problem?" Ivy asked Fiona. She still had to fix her hair.

Fiona stuck out her tongue. Madison grinned.

"I feel different now," Lindsay said, sitting on her bag to zip it up.

"Me too," Madison whispered. All packed and ready to go. She pulled her baseball cap onto her head.

Stacey and Aimee swept the floor, not because it was a little dirty after two nights of mud and rain—but because it was a requested chore. The camp staff and FHJH teachers had composed a brief list of "other things to do" before the field trip ended. The list had been attached to the original agenda. Madison wondered why they couldn't attend any school event without a bunch of rules.

Afternoon of Departure

1. Sweep the cabin, deck of cabin, and walkway near cabin. Floor should not have pine needles, dust, caked dirt, or anything else on it.
2. Remove any litter from barrel near door. There is a main Dumpster near main lodge.
3. Remove all sheets and other materials from the mattresses. Pack with your belongings.
4. Double-check bathroom cabin for shampoo, soap, and other personal belongings.
5. Refrain from carving or writing your names into the rafters or anywhere else in the room.

Having finished their packing, Rose and Joan perched on their beds and carved their names into one of the beams in Maple cabin. Madison was a little jealous of the drones. Everyone else wanted to leave her name behind, too, but there wasn't enough time.

"You guys, we have only ten minutes to get our stuff out of here," Fiona announced. "It looks like everyone else really is on their way to the main lodge. . . ."

"Stop nagging everyone," Ivy moaned.

Fiona stuck out her tongue behind Ivy's back again and slammed the screen door.

The girls left their suitcases and duffel bags on the cabin stoop and trudged over to the main lodge for the final lunch. Madison pulled her orange bag containing her notebook, her wallet, and a few other items over her shoulder. She stuffed her fleece into the bag, too, in case she needed it.

Fiona was wrong about Maple cabin being the last to go to lunch. The boys were on the path, too. Madison walked alongside Dan and Egg.

"Congrats on your climb," Dan said.

"Yeah, Maddie, you aced that Tower," Egg said. "I thought you said you were scared."

"You didn't look scared," Dan said.

Madison smiled. "I was," she admitted. "But I did it, anyway."

Egg slapped her on the back. "Wasn't it worth having a total anxiety attack over? Huh? Huh? Wasn't it worth it?"

Madison chuckled, but Egg was right. It *was* worth it. The entire field trip had been worth all of its anxiety and pressure. This really was one of those "growing experiences" Principal Bernard had talked about.

The only possible drawback to the end of the field trip for Madison was giving up on her crush, Hart, who seemed to prefer Ivy's company. A few paces ahead of Madison, Hart was walking to the lodge with the enemy right now.

But Madison refused to believe that she'd lost Hart to Ivy forever. One day she'd admit her real feelings to Hart's face. *One day.*

When they walked inside the main lodge, Madison and her friends smelled the clipped daffodils, hyacinth, and other wildflowers that had bloomed early in Jasper Woods. A large sign hung over the front doors that read, THANK U, CAMPERS! Everyone hustled inside and took their seats.

"I'm hungry!" Dan said.

"Yeah, like that's a surprise," Aimee said.

There was a buffet of sandwiches, chips, brownies, and a big bowl of cold oranges. Much to Madison's delight, they had put out cans of soda, including root beer. Everyone got their food and sat boy-girl-boy-girl at the tables.

"Well," Mrs. Goode said, her voice booming as usual. "I want to congratulate all of you on a very successful field trip. The camp director tells me that you are the finest group of seventh graders she has had in some time."

Pam, who was standing next to Mrs. Goode, nodded and clapped.

"Wawooooo!" someone yelled. The room burst into laughter that quickly escalated into loud chatter.

"Students! Students!" Mrs. Goode continued.

"As you know, we have a few awards of recognition we need to distribute."

The same kid yelled, "Wawooooo!" again.

"First!" Mrs. Goode said. "Mr. Danehy and the other science teachers would like to present some awards for our junior naturalists, otherwise known as our scavenger hunt winners."

Mr. Danehy, wearing an ecology club T-shirt that read ECOLOGY 4-EVER, stepped into the center of the room.

"You all did a tremendous job of gathering the objects on the list," Mr. Danehy said. "Unfortunately, there can be only one grand-prize trophy winner."

"They always say that," Egg moaned. He was ultracompetitive.

"But we have ribbons for all runners-up," Mr. Danehy continued.

There were eleven teams in all. He read off the names of the team members slowly, which was irritating at first. But then Madison and her friends realized that after nine teams, they still hadn't been named.

"I bet we won," Drew said.

"We totally won," Chet said.

The table held their collective breath.

"And in second place," Mr. Danehy cried, "Walter Diaz, Madison Finn . . ."

"Practically first," Madison said.

Fiona sighed. "We deserve more than just a

150

ribbon. It's no fair that those boys get the trophies."

"Come on, we did great," Dan said, giving his guy friends high fives.

"It was your sleeping bag that got us into the top two, Aim," Egg joked, elbowing Aimee in the side.

"Shut up!" Aimee said, laughing. She smacked his arm.

"Hey, second place is better than Ivy did," Lindsay whispered to Madison.

"Now!" Mrs. Goode continued. "Before we move on to the talent show prizes, I have another special trophy here for . . ." She checked her notes. "For the best time on our obstacle course."

Hart leaned forward. He was hoping his time would be the best.

"With a running time of three minutes and twenty-six seconds, the winner of the obstacle course is . . . Wayne Ennis!"

Egg's jaw dropped. "There must be a mistake," he said.

Madison whacked his arm. "Shhh!" she said.

Hart dropped his head. "Crud," he said.

"Sorry," Madison said.

"Yeah, thanks," Hart replied, still looking down.

Madison had never seen him bummed out like this before.

Meanwhile Egg, Chet, Dan, and Drew were all making each other laugh with bad imitations of Wayne accepting his trophy.

"Shhhhh!" Madison said again. She didn't want Egg to get into trouble.

"And now on to our fabulous talent show. And I must start out by saying that the faculty and the camp staff were *all* impressed with your various performances. We have divided the talent show awards into categories. Everyone who participated receives a prize," Mrs. Goode explained. "And then we have extra-special recognition and three trophies for all-around talent."

"Huh?" Aimee said. "She makes it sound so complicated."

"Yeah," Lindsay added. "It's not the Academy Awards."

Fiona giggled.

Madison was taking it a little more seriously than her other three friends. She gripped tightly under the bench where she was sitting. She really wanted to win a prize for the talent show performance. This was the place where beating Ivy really mattered. The BFFs had to win one of the trophies.

Mrs. Goode read off a bunch of fun categories of recognition like "Happiest Song and Dance" and "Best Crowd Pleaser." These were joke categories as far as most kids were concerned. It was just the school's way of giving everyone a little something, even if they were really bad.

"For 'Most Creative Use of Props,'" Mrs. Goode announced, "we have The Dudes."

Egg stood up and whirled his fist in the air. "Duuuuuude!" he cried. The room broke into laughter. His team won the last of the special categories. Now, it was on to the trophies.

Madison held her breath. She looked over at Fiona, Aimee, and Lindsay expectantly. They all grabbed hands.

"Third place in the 'All-Around' category goes to . . ."

Madison gulped.

"The BFFs!"

She sighed. A well of emotion surged through her chest. *Third* place? It meant that Ivy's group had gotten second or first. It meant they got the smallest of the three trophies.

Madison was disappointed, but Lindsay jumped right up, squealing.

"Coolness!" Lindsay shouted. She grabbed the other girls and they accepted their trophies. Madison smiled as much as she could under the circumstances.

"Grrrr . . . It was those minishorts," Aimee said. "I swear, it is so unfair how she wins all the time. Why does that happen?"

Madison shrugged. At least Ivy hadn't climbed the tower first, too. Madison would always have that honor.

Thankfully, Ivy and Sweet Stuff collected second place. They'd won a bigger trophy—but not the biggest. First prize went to a group of boys who called themselves Funk. They had performed some kind of special techno-dance with somersaults and harmonized melodies. They really had been the best.

Everyone in the room clapped, thinking that the ceremonies had ended. But Mrs. Goode waved her arms.

"Hold on," she cried. "We have a few more announcements. Please take your seats. This year we decided to distribute a few additional awards for recognition on the field trip. These students receive a special certificate. Mrs. Wing, would you do the honors?"

Madison picked a chocolate chip off her brownie. What would they give Ivy this time—an award for best kiss-up?

"For 'Best Leader,'" Mrs. Wing said, "we have a three-way tie. Walter Diaz, Lois Gillooly, and Juliette Rothwax."

Madison clapped politely. She grinned at Egg, who was bouncing off the walls.

"I got a special award," he exclaimed. "Now *this* is cool! I'm king of the world!"

Everyone laughed, as usual, at Egg's dramatics.

"For 'Best Athlete,'" Mrs. Wing said, "we have a two-way tie. Hart Jones and Fiona Waters."

Fiona's eyes opened wide. She hadn't expected to win anything. Hart jumped up and grabbed his award, too.

Madison smiled at Hart, but he was too busy looking around the room to notice. She checked to make sure he wasn't smiling at Ivy instead. Thankfully, he wasn't.

Mrs. Wing read through a few other awards for "Best Entertainer," "Best Cabin Buddy," "Best Tower Climber," and more. Most awards had two-way, three-way, and even four-way ties. Everyone was recognized in some way.

"And for 'best Camp Spirit,'" Mrs. Wing said, "we have a two-way tie. Dan Ginsburg and Madison Finn."

Mrs. Wing beamed brightly as she handed Madison her certificate.

"Congratulations," Mrs. Wing whispered. "Good job."

Madison's stomach flip-flopped—but in a good way.

"Hey, Maddie," Fiona whispered. "Camp spirit . . . like the haunted cabin ghost?"

Madison laughed. "Yeah, right." She read the certificate at least ten more times before placing it inside her orange bag.

"Congrats, Maddie," Dan said.

"You too," Madison said. Dan looked proud of his certificate, too.

After the lunch ended, the seventh grade broke into a chorus of "On Top of Spaghetti." Everyone gathered together and headed out to the lawn behind the lodge for arts and crafts before the buses took them home. Since it was such a nice afternoon, they did their last activity outdoors.

"What is this?" Egg asked. "I feel like I'm in kindergarten, making a gift for my mom like a souvenir of camp or something."

Drew snorted. "That's funny, Egg."

But Madison wasn't laughing. She was excited about this part of the day. Making art was something she really loved—something she was good at.

The camp staff and FHJH teachers put out various supplies like glue, paper plates, string, and scissors for the students' use. On one table were the piles of items retrieved from the scavenger hunt, except for Aimee's sleeping bag, of course. She'd gotten that returned to her right after the contest.

Nothing was mandatory. If kids didn't want to make crafts, they didn't have to. Some chose to draw or sketch. Some wrote in their own journals. Madison saw that she wasn't the only one who had come armed with a notebook.

And some kids did nothing but sit. Like Ivy and the drones. They sat under a tree, off to the side, gossiping and acting as exclusive as ever.

Fiona, Aimee, and Lindsay each grabbed a paper plate and plopped down on the grass. They wanted to make M.A.S.H. charts again. But Madison wanted to make something else—something that would be a souvenir for herself. Collages were her thing, even if they were composed of flat stones and blades of grass instead of words and pictures from magazines.

After a half hour, a loud horn blared. Mrs. Goode clapped and asked everyone to line up for the departure from camp.

Madison shoved her decorated plate into her orange bag, which was overflowing by now. She looked up at the blue sky over Jasper Woods for the last time and sucked in some of the warm afternoon air. Off in the distance, the Tower rose up from the ground in the distance, orange and imposing.

But this was nothing to fear—not anymore.

She noticed that Fiona, Aimee, and Lindsay had grabbed their stuff and were heading for the bus line.

"Hey, wait for me!" Madison cried, waving.

"Wait!" Aimee said. "We have one more thing to do before we get on the bus."

Fiona grinned. She tugged Madison's sleeve, pulling her along.

"What?" Madison asked.

Lindsay had to stifle a giggle, too.

"What is this?" Madison asked again. "We'll be late. . . ."

Aimee and the others led Madison over to the Tower, the site of Madison's morning triumph. They bent down.

"Look," Aimee said. "Here!" She pointed to one of the beams along the Tower's base.

Madison wrinkled her brow. "So?" she said, leaning closer to the base.

There, in the middle of one beam, she saw what her friends wanted her to see. Carved into the wood was a simple message:

M. F. + A. G. + F. W. + L. F.
4-EVER

The bus sounded like a camp song jukebox that had short-circuited. Kids were singing at least four different songs at once. But as discordant as it sounded, the bus was a happy place to be sitting right now. And it was much less cliquey than it had been on the trip out to Jasper Woods.

Plus, Madison loved it because now she knew most of the songs.

"'Miss Lucy had a steamboat, the steamboat had a bell, Miss Lucy went to heaven, but the steamboat went to . . .'"

"HELL-O, operator!" Egg cried.

Mrs. Goode stood up, clapping. "Okay, we're heading back to Far Hills. The trip takes about three hours from here. I want all of you to behave, please, on the ride back. We will be stopping at designated school bus stops that were prearranged by your parents. We'll also be stopping back at the main school building. A parent must be there to take you home."

Everyone kept on singing for a good ten minutes, but after that some kids stopped to talk. Others closed their eyes and napped. Madison yawned. It had been an exhausting three days.

Hart sat in the back of the bus near Ivy again, but he spent most of the time goofing off with Chet, so Madison wasn't too jealous. Ivy and the drones kept mostly to themselves.

Aimee proudly showed off the results of her newest M.A.S.H. chart, which she'd finished after boarding the bus. Her future destiny was revealed. She would be a prima ballerina, riding in her limousine, living in a mansion in Paris, honeymooning in Tahiti, and having two kids.

"You cheated," Madison said. "That's too perfect."

"You can't cheat fate," Aimee said, smiling.

Fiona showed the results of her M.A.S.H. quiz. Fiona was an archaeologist, riding on a donkey, living in the woods in an apartment, honeymooning in Far Hills, and having 99 kids.

"Hey, you and Maddie both have ninety-nine kids," Lindsay said, laughing.

"Now, *that's* more like it," Madison said. "See, Aimee? Fiona's is better."

"And what's wrong with that?" Aimee said.

Fiona reread her results. "Do they have apartments in the woods? A donkey? Gosh, my future is scary."

The BFFs laughed together.

"What about you, Lindsay?" Madison asked.

Lindsay hadn't finished hers. "I'm too superstitious," she said. "What if it really did come true? That's too weird for me."

The girls talked about the homework that was due the following Monday and gossiped about the boys a little, but eventually, each of them dozed off. Madison was going to write in her notebook, but she decided to wait until she got home to her laptop.

By the time the bus arrived back at FHJH, it was dark outside.

As she got in her mom's car, Ivy glared at Madison with piercing eyes that told Madison it wasn't ever going to be over between them. Their feud was one sure thing that didn't change at camp, Madison thought. Standing by the bus, she watched Ivy get smaller and smaller as Mrs. Daly drove away.

The remaining BFFs quickly spotted Mr. Waters. He stood waiting by the family minivan.

"Your chauffeur is here!" he joked as the three girls and Chet climbed inside.

"Oh, Dad," Fiona gushed. Chet hopped into the front. Madison, Aimee, and Fiona went into the back.

When Mr. Waters pulled up in front of Madison's house, Madison grabbed her heavy orange bag and climbed out.

"Let's all meet up in the chat room tonight?" Madison asked her friends.

"Around nine?" Fiona asked.

"It's a date!" Aimee said. "If I don't crash earlier."

As Madison climbed the porch steps, the tiredness from the field trip hit her all at once.

"Rowwrooooooo!" Phin barked from behind the front door. Madison could hear his little nails clickety-clicking. He had been watching her through the window as she came up the front walk.

"Phinnie!" Madison cried, flinging open the door. She collapsed on the rug. He licked her ears.

"Is that you, Maddie?" Mom called out. She had on her jacket and the car keys were in hand. "Welcome back, honey bear. How was it?"

Madison sighed. She held up a single finger as if to say, "Hold on a sec," and opened up her orange bag. Phin nipped at her knees.

"This is how it was, Mom," Madison said, producing the certificate for "Best Camp Spirit."

"Wow," Mom said. She kissed Madison on the nose. "Let me look at you. You look the same. Oh, wait a minute! I see a new gleam in your eye. . . ."

"Quit it, Mom," Madison said, giggling.

"I'm so proud of you," Mom said, rereading the award certificate.

"It's not a big deal in the world or anything, but . . ." Madison's voice trailed off. "I don't know. It is a big deal to me. I won something."

"Yes, it *is* a big deal," Mom said. "Okay, I should dash to the gas station and pick up dinner. I hope pizza is okay. Didn't have time to cook. I'll be back in a flash. We can talk more later."

Madison gave Mom a big hug. "I missed you."

"Phinnie slept on your bed every night," Mom said. "We missed you, too."

Madison leaned down to hold Phin close. "Good boy," she cooed into his little pug ears.

Mom ran out the door and Madison threw her stuff to the side of the hallway. She'd unpack later.

She had said her hellos to two of the three things she missed most. Dog, Mom, and now . . . Madison needed to reunite with the laptop. She pulled off her sneakers and ran in her socks up to the bedroom.

Hummmnummmm.

The laptop hummed as she turned it on. She punched the keys to log online and waited for a connection. There wasn't as much e-mail as she'd expected, but it was from some of her favorite people.

FROM	SUBJECT
✉ JeffFinn	STILL SICK
✉ Bigwheels	He's Back!
✉ GoGramma	Miss You
✉ W_Wonka7	Photos 4 Everyone

Still sick? Poor Dad. Madison opened his e-mail first.

From: JeffFinn
To: MadFinn
Subject: STILL SICK
Date: Fri 25 April 5:45 PM
_____
Hey, Maddie . . . TOY! It's Friday,
and I'm here in my pajamas with a
very red nose.

Is it tonight that your class comes
home or tomorrow? I can't remember.
Could be the flu medicine I've been
taking. But I'm getting better
slowly. Fever isn't so bad. Let's
try to have dinner Monday or
Tuesday night with Stephanie. She
wants to see you.

Hey, did u hear about the sick
ghost? He had an oooooooo-ping
cough. LOL. Thought you'd like that
one.

I can't wait to hear how everything
went @ Jasper Woods. I haven't been
up there in years. And you're a
born camper, Maddie! Dads know these
things.

ILY,

Dad

Madison hit REPLY and sent Dad a get-well-soon wish. Then she opened the next e-mail, from Gramma Helen. It felt so good to be back online.

```
From: GoGramma
To: MadFinn
Subject: Miss You
Date: Fri 25 April 7:04 PM
```

Hello, my dear. I just got off the telephone with your mother who tells me you're still off camping with the seventh grade. Well, good for you! I'm sure there was nothing to worry about. Were Aimee and Fiona there?

Have you and your mom planted the flowers in the backyard yet?

Call me on Sunday so we can chat. Give Phin a hug, too.

Love,

Gramma

Madison grabbed a piece of paper from her desk and scribbled *Gramma* on top so she'd remember to call the next day. Then she moved to the next e-mail, from her keypal.

From: Bigwheels
To: MadFinn
Subject: He's Back!
Date: Sat 26 April 9:10 AM

I am such a spaz! I looked 4 u
online all day Thursday to chat and
was sad when I couldn't find u n e
where. But it's ur school field
trip. U get back tonight, right?
How did it go?

Here's the best news in the world.
Reggie said he was sorry. I was
like, TAH! But then he kept calling
Thurs. night and then all day in
school Fri. and I still like him.
So we're back together. He's sooo
. . . he even gave me some daisies.
Did Hart ever give u daisies? That
means he likes me again, right? I
took one from the bunch and did
that "loves me, loves me not" game.
Guess which one came up?

I hate it when we're not e-mailing.
Let's go online & chat tomorrow. I
MISS U!!!!!!!

Yours till the gum balls,

Victoria, aka Bigwheels

166

Madison saved Bigwheels' message in her files. It was a relief to know that Reggie was back on the scene. Madison hated sad endings to love stories, especially when her own love life was such a question mark.

She wanted to get through all the e-mails before responding to Bigwheels, so Madison clicked on the message from W_Wonka7. That was Drew. He'd sent it only moments earlier.

```
From: W_Wonka7
To: LuvNstuff, MadFinn, BalletGrl,
Wetwin, Wetwinz, Sk8ingboy,
TheEggMan, Dantheman
Subject: Photos 4 Everyone
Date: Sat 26 April 6:55 PM
```
Hey, there. I took some kool shots of everyone @ camp and on the bus. My digital camera rocks.

:>)))))

C U in school on Monday!

Drew

<attachment:JASPERWOODS>

<attachment:ONTHEBUS>

<attachment:THETOWER>

Madison clicked open the attachments from Drew's e-mail. In the first photo, Drew and the boys were goofing off in front of their cabin. Hart looked as cute as ever. Madison saved it to disk so she could print it out later on Mom's laser printer.

The photo from the bus was a shot of everyone all squished together, arms waving. Egg was making a funny face. Dan had rabbit ears pointed behind Aimee's head. Fiona and Chet were wrestling to be in front. Madison was off to the side, near Hart.

Hart. Sigh.

But the last photo was the best of all.

Drew had taken a digital shot of everyone cheering on while someone climbed the Tower. That person was Madison. He'd angled the camera so that Madison looked like a real daredevil, half hanging off the side of a beam. She had one arm raised in the air—like Madison the Conqueror. In the picture, Madison was beaming under her orange helmet.

From under the desk, Phin nuzzled Madison's feet.

"I did it, Phinnie," Madison said, kissing the top of his head. "I made it."

Madison leaned over and opened up her bag. It was like a bag of camp memories. First, she took out the Camp Spirit certificate. She could scan it into her files to save and e-mail to Gramma Helen and Dad. Then she would find a frame to hang it over her desk. Next, Madison gently pulled out the paper-plate collage she'd made that afternoon. One corner got squished on the journey home, but it still looked pretty enough. She would give that to Mom at dinner. Finally, Madison pulled out her Day-Glo orange notebook and flipped through the pages. Reading it was like being at camp all over again. She powered up her laptop and began to type the notebook entries into her computer files.

"Maddie!" Mom yelled from downstairs. "Are you up there? Maddie! Pizza's here! Hungry?"

"I'm coming, Mom!" Madison cried, quickly shutting her computer down.

Madison closed her notebook and sighed. She was no longer the camp outsider. She had survived Ivy, mud, and the Tower. She really *was* Madison the conqueror.

Mad chat Words:

```
:-e        Totally disappointed
>^,,^<     Kitty cat
:>))))     Very, very, VERY happy
HAGO       Have a good one
LOL        Laughing out loud
LYL        Love you lots
Fotos      Photographs
TAH        Take a hike
Pleez      Please
TOY        Thinking of you
SoooS      So-o-o sweet
ILY        I love you
```

Madison's Computer Tip

Going away to camp was a good experience in more ways than one. Of course it was great because I did a bunch of things I didn't expect to do, like climb that Tower and even perform in the talent show. At first I was devastated that I couldn't get e-mail or search the Internet or chat on bigfishbowl.com. But everything worked out. **I realize that being on the computer 24/7 isn't good for anyone**. My three-day break from my laptop with the orange notebook was fun. Sometimes I waste time getting online when I should have more face time with my friends. That's what this field trip was really about.

Visit Madison at www.madisonfinn.com